'What a transformation!'

Simon looked her up and down appreciatively. 'You ought to wear your hair loose more often. I like it a lot better than that prim little knob you wore on top of your head when we first met. I'm sure you're not really prim.' He hesitated, then added with a twinkle, 'Well, fairly sure!'

Wendy laughed and felt herself colouring, but she did not take up the challenge he had offered her.

Dear Reader,

Practice Nurse Amy Kincaid finds that she is IN
SAFE HANDS in Margaret O'Neill's latest GP story,
while Canadian physiotherapist Jane Easter tries to
convince Dirk that the unknown can exist in Sara
Burton's BEYOND HEAVEN AND EARTH. A convalescent home is the unusual setting for Clare
Lavenham's offering in SISTER AT HILLSIDE, and
the beautiful Great Barrier Reef is the backdrop for
Judith Worthy's STORM IN PARADISE.

Travel the world without leaving home!

The Editor

Clare Lavenham was a Londoner, but has lived
mostly in Suffolk. She is widowed with two grown-
up children. She has written articles, short stories
and one-act plays, but her work as a hospital librarian
led to her writing Medical Romances. She gets her
backgrounds from her library work, and consults
various medical friends when necessary. Her favourite occupations, apart from writing, are walking in
the country and gardening.

Recent titles by the same author:

WIND OF CHANGE
.OVE YOUR NEIGHBOUR

SISTER AT HILLSIDE

BY

CLARE LAVENHAM

MILLS & BOON LIMITED
ETON HOUSE   18–24 PARADISE ROAD
RICHMOND   SURREY   TW9 1SR

First published in Great Britain 1992
by Mills & Boon Limited

© Clare Lavenham 1992

Australian copyright 1992
Philippine copyright 1992
This edition 1992

ISBN 0 263 77918 1

Set in 10½ on 12½ pt Linotron Palatino
03-9211-45414

Typeset in Great Britain by Centracet, Cambridge
Made and printed in Great Britain

CHAPTER ONE

IT WAS very quiet in the small, cramped office crowded with books, files and odd pieces of medical equipment. Wendy could hear birds singing in the tall trees outside, but the only sound indoors was the hum of an electric polisher in the corridor.

Miss Lavinia Greenfield, the nursing officer who was sister-in-charge at Hillside Convalescent Home, was studying some notes on the desk, but now she looked up suddenly and fixed Wendy with a penetrating stare from pale blue eyes behind bifocal glasses.

'I see from your CV, Nurse McBride, that you've been working as a staff nurse at Benham Hospital, but you scarcely look old enough——'

'I'm twenty-four, and I've been a staff nurse for three years.'

'Really?' A faint smile softened the thin face. 'I would have taken you for no more than twenty.'

Wendy knew she looked young, and it had always been a trial to her. Only five foot three and very slender, she usually wore her dark gold hair in a pony tail, but today she had screwed it up into a small knob on top of her head, hoping it would make her look older and more worthy of responsibility. Apparently the attempt had failed.

'We don't have staff nurses here,' Miss Greenfield went on. 'Only two of our nurses are fully qualified, and they're both sisters, while the others are mostly part-time middle-aged women who trained as state-enrolled nurses some time ago. They're all excellent workers, and I have the utmost confidence in them.'

Wendy listened with a sinking heart. It didn't look as though she was going to get the job, and she wanted it very badly.

'I don't mind working with older women—provided they have no objection to working with *me*,' she said. 'How old is the sister who's leaving?'

'About thirty, and the other one is the same age.'

'I shall be twenty-five in August, and I've had plenty of very varied experience. I often took charge of the ward when Sister was off duty.' Unconsciously, Wendy tilted her chin and met the nursing officer's doubtful gaze with a defiant stare from hazel eyes flecked with green.

'I don't doubt your qualifications, Nurse,' Miss Greenfield said quietly, 'but there's one other matter—apart from your youthfulness—which is worrying me. I feel you may be imagining that working in a convalescent home is an easy, comfortable job, but I assure you that at times it can be tough and difficult, even involving a certain amount of lifting.'

She looked searchingly at the delicate-featured

face opposite, and Wendy was conscious of blue-shadowed eyes and a general air of fragility.

'I've only just got over an accident,' she hurried to explain. 'A bad car crash——'

Suddenly she was back in the not-very-distant past, to that terrible day when she had been driving her Mini along a busy motorway with her fiancé as passenger, and suddenly a vehicle had come hurtling across the central reservation. It was a big red car and it had come straight towards the tiny Mini with the inevitability of a thunderbolt. There was no time to take avoiding action, no time for anything, not even a prayer.

Wendy could still remember the awful noise of shattering glass and crumpling metal—she didn't think she would ever forget it—and then everything went black.

She came to, hours later, in a hospital bed, with her mother sitting beside her. There was pain in every limb and her head ached unbearably. The sister appeared and told her she had several fractured ribs, concussion and a badly sprained ankle, but on the whole she had come off lightly. When she asked about Vernon they told her, very gently and kindly, that he was dead.

Miss Greenfield cleared her throat and said sympathetically, 'I can see it still haunts you, and no doubt you're longing to get back to work in the hope of erasing the memory, but are you sure you're strong enough?'

'My family doctor said it would be all right——'

no need to mention that she'd talked him into it '—and, though I know I still look a bit fragile, I feel OK—honestly!'

The nursing officer smiled at her vehemence. 'I must admit we do need someone urgently, and I suppose you'd be able to start quite soon?'

'Any time! I gave in my notice at Benham as soon as I decided to have a change,' Wendy told her.

'It would certainly be a great advantage to appoint someone who's free from other commitments. The sister whom you would replace is anxious to leave as soon as possible so as to be able to look after her mother, who's unfortunately terminally ill.'

She leaned back in her chair and stared thoughtfully out of the window. Following her gaze, Wendy saw a wide expanse of grass with flowerbeds along the nearer edge. They were bright with primulas, tulips and forget-me-nots, all very neat and well cared for, and for the first time she became fully aware of the loveliness of Hillside and a faint stirring of enthusiasm within herself.

She wanted the job—wanted it badly—but all her reasons had been unconnected with the job itself.

Although it was only a few seconds, it seemed a long time before Miss Greenfield resumed the conversation. Wendy tried to wait patiently, but her hands were twisting together in her lap and her heart was beating faster than normal. It was a relief when she found herself once more under scrutiny, and guessed from the nursing officer's face that she had made up her mind.

'Well, Nurse McBride, I've decided to recommend to the authorities that you be given the post. As I've already warned you, you may find certain difficulties at first, but I'm hoping you have the determination to overcome them.' She stood up abruptly. 'And now I expect you'd like to look round.'

The cleaner with her polisher had gone, and the only person they met in the corridor was a girl in a primrose-coloured button-through dress. She had a plait of red hair and bright blue eyes which eyed the stranger with frank curiosity.

'I forgot to mention,' Miss Greenfield said, 'that in addition to the nurses we also have a number of teenagers who divide their time between a pre-nursing course at Stourwell College and helping us here.' Her lips twisted into a rueful smile. 'Sometimes they're quite useful—and quite often just the opposite. Most of the older patients like them because they're young and lively and usually have time to spare.'

They passed through some swing doors and entered a large black-and-white-tiled hall from which an elegant curving staircase rose to the first floor. Hillside had once been a stately home, though a very minor one, and it retained a great many of its original features.

A group of female patients, sitting round a low

table and talking or knitting, glanced up with mild interest, but a row of elderly men against the wall sat staring into space with unoccupied hands and—apparently—empty minds.

'It's so difficult to get the men interested in anything,' the sister-in-charge said in a low voice. 'The occupational therapist comes out twice a week from the City Hospital, but she doesn't have much success with our male patients.'

She opened a door and briefly displayed a pleasant dining-room with french windows. Next to it was the so-called quiet room, where one wall was taken up by a big bookcase with glass doors, and the third door led into a lounge with television and a piano. Both these rooms also had french windows opening into the park.

Upstairs there were several large bedrooms which had been made into miniature wards, all with a magnificent view. There must be another floor above, Wendy reasoned, but she was not shown it.

'Where do the staff live?' she asked when she had admired the newly modernised bath and shower-rooms.

'Mostly on the second floor, where I have a flat, but the two sisters are lodged outside the main building. They each have a flatlet made out of the upper floor of what used to be the head gardener's cottage, not far from the entrance gates.'

'What's the ground floor of the cottage used for?' Wendy enquired with idle curiosity.

'That's also a flat, though the original kitchen has been turned into a laundry-room which is used by all three tenants. Dr Meadows lives there.'

'I suppose he—or she—is the resident physician here?'

'Oh, no, we don't have a doctor of our own. There wouldn't be nearly enough for him to do. Simon Meadows is a registrar on the medical side at the main hospital, but he looks after Hillside as well.'

'Surely it's a bit inconvenient for him, living so far out of the city?' Wendy ventured to comment.

'It's not as far as you seem to imagine. The hospital is this side of the city, you know, and he can be there in less than ten minutes if he's summoned for an emergency.' Miss Greenfield paused at the top of the stairs and looked rather doubtfully at the slim, pale-faced girl following her. 'Am I right in thinking you don't have a car?'

Wendy shook her head. 'Not now,' she said briefly.

Whether the nursing officer guessed she had been driving her own car when she was involved in the accident, she had no means of telling, but at least Miss Greenfield did not ask any further questions.

'Both the present sisters have cars,' she went on, 'and no doubt Sister Templeton would be glad to give you a lift into the city sometimes. I believe there's also a bus, but I don't know anything about its reliability.'

'Surely we couldn't both be off duty at the same time?' Wendy exclaimed.

'I have no objection in the afternoon, provided I'm here myself. They're both off duty now, by the way, or I would have introduced you.' Miss Greenfield paused to hold open the swing doors for an old man struggling through with two sticks. 'And now come along back to the office and I'll organise a cup of tea for us. Have you arranged for a taxi to call for you?'

'I didn't know what time I'd get away.' Wendy rummaged in her bag. 'I've got a list of trains.'

Seated alone in the office while Miss Greenfield went along to the kitchen, she was consulting her list when there was a tap on the door, which immediately opened, and a broad-shouldered, brown-haired young man looked in.

'Hello!' He stared at the occupant in surprise. 'Where's Miss Greenfield?'

'Ordering tea.'

'Great! I'm just in time for a cuppa.' He sat down and stretched out his long legs, looking very much at home. 'I'm not supposed to know you, am I?'

She shook her head. 'I'm Wendy McBride, and I hope I'm going to take the place of the sister who's leaving.'

'Simon Meadows.' He stood up again and enveloped her small hand in a warm, firm clasp.

Retrieving it, Wendy reflected—absurdly—that she now knew how Jonah had felt when being swallowed by the whale. Her lips twitched and she could see he was wondering what had amused her.

She said hastily, 'You must be the registrar who takes care of the patients here and lives in the gardener's cottage.'

'I see my fame has preceded me!'

They both laughed, and Wendy allowed herself to study him from beneath her lashes as he re-seated himself. She saw that his brown hair had a reddish gleam and his eyes were a strange tawny shade with thick brown lashes. His face was squarish, with a strong jawline and a wide, generous mouth. Although it was only the end of April, his clear skin was lightly tanned, and she could imagine him tramping through the countryside at weekends and maybe playing a lot of tennis.

At that moment Miss Greenfield returned, followed by a member of the kitchen staff with a tea tray.

'I'll fetch another cup,' the girl said, smiling at Simon.

He was politely on his feet again, but the nursing officer waved him back to his chair, complimenting him as she did so on his clever timing.

'I hoped I might have got it right.' He suddenly became businesslike. 'I hear you've had a spot of bother with Mrs Porter?'

'She had another slight stroke this morning and seems rather poorly, so we had to keep her in bed. It's very disappointing, because she was doing so well and hoped to go home on Sunday.'

'I'll go up and take a look at her when I've had my tea.'

The extra cup had arrived and Miss Greenfield began to pour out. 'I suppose you two have introduced yourselves?' she said.

It was Simon who confirmed it. He glanced at Wendy as he spoke and, although his words had been formally polite, she was startled to catch a glimpse of a disturbing expression in his eyes. It vanished almost immediately, but in her own mind she could only describe it as uneasy. Perhaps even critical.

Her new-found confidence was nearly shattered, and only the thought that her appointment to the post of sister at Hillside had nothing to do with Simon Meadows restored her sufficiently to re-enter the conversation and ask if she might use the phone to order a taxi.

'Of course you can.' The nursing officer hesitated. 'Are you going straight back to the hospital, Simon?'

'Yes, indeed—we're very busy. Why?' He raised thickly marked brows and looked at her enquiringly.

'Nurse McBride has to return to Benham by train. I was wondering whether you could give her a lift to the station?'

'With pleasure,' he said courteously and, Wendy was sure, with complete insincerity. 'In about fifteen minutes?'

'That would fit in very well with my train,'

Wendy said, and added with a politeness which matched his, 'If you're sure it's no trouble? I don't want to take you out of your way.'

'It'll be OK as long as we get away from here before the rush-hour starts.' He got up and made for the door. 'I'd better go and see Mrs Porter.'

Miss Greenfield accompanied him, and Wendy, left alone, went to stare out of the window. Everywhere there were signs that summer was waiting on the threshold. The roses in a large circular bed were in full leaf and, at the far end of the lawn, a huge bank of glossy-leaved rhododendrons was already showing promise of imminent flowering—pink, white and scarlet. They would be a wonderful sight in a couple of weeks.

Would she be here to see them?

Simon's car was small and sporty-looking. Its colour appeared to be metallic blue, but a great deal of it was obscured by mud. He drove down the short drive at a good speed and shot past a small gabled house standing at a little distance.

'Is that where you live?' Wendy asked, looking at it with interest since, if all went well, it would soon be her own home as well.

'Yes.' He paused fractionally, then swung out on to the road. 'I'm very lucky not to have to live in the hospital. Out here I can go jogging straight from my own front door.'

'I get the impression you're a bit of a sports freak,' she commented.

'Not really. I just like to keep healthy, that's all. I was brought up on a farm and I don't like being shut up indoors too much.'

'Medicine isn't exactly an outdoor profession. Did you never consider taking up farming yourself?'

'Never. My mother is a doctor, and it's in my blood much more than farming is. Besides, I have an elder brother who's working with my father and will take over when he retires.'

They had already left the country behind and were driving through residential streets. Feeling she had done her share of keeping the conversation going, Wendy subsided into silence. She had an uneasy feeling that Dr Meadows was regarding the drive to the station as a tiresome chore which had been thrust upon him. In view of the fact that they would very likely soon become near neighbours, she thought he might have shown a little more interest.

Stourwell was a cathedral city and had managed to retain some of the elegance associated with such places. There were half-timbered houses and Georgian terraces mixed in with more modern buildings which had been carefully vetted by the planners. The area round the cathedral itself was still a tangle of medieval lanes.

Wendy gazed about her with pleasure, hoping that before long she would get a chance to explore. It was extraordinary that she should know so little about the place, since Benham was only fifty miles away.

Apart from short local trips, she had mostly used her car for taking her widowed mother and her grandmother, who lived with them, for drives, and they had both preferred the sea. Even when she got engaged to Vernon, they did not do much motoring because he was temporarily without a car, having been banned for a year owing to having failed the breathalyser. The motorway accident had been particularly unfortunate because they were only on one because of a long-standing invitation to visit mutual friends.

'What time is your train?' Simon asked abruptly as they followed the one-way system round the market place.

'Sixteen-twenty. Is it much further to the station?'

'Oh, no—we'll be there in a few minutes——'

He broke off and put his foot down sharply on the brake as a car drew out from a parking space by the kerb right in their path. Wendy, jerked violently forward, felt her seatbelt tighten instantly, but could not entirely stifle a scream of terror. She was conscious of a cold sweat on her forehead and hoped desperately she wouldn't disgrace herself by fainting.

'Bloody fool!' muttered Simon as he miraculously avoided a collision. He turned his head and glanced at his passenger. 'At least it wasn't a woman driver!' His tone changed. 'I say, are you all right?'

'Yes, thanks.' Wendy struggled to justify a greenish-white face and terror-stricken eyes. 'Just for a second I thought we were going to crash right into him.'

'Serve him right if we had, but I don't want my own car messed up.' He gave her another worried glance. 'Are you sure you feel OK?'

'I do now.'

She supposed she ought to offer an explanation for over-reacting like that, but before she could embark on it Simon turned a corner and pointed ahead.

'There you are—there's the station. You've got plenty of time.'

It was obviously too late now to tell him about the terrible accident she'd been involved in so recently. Wendy thanked him politely for the lift, got out as quickly as possible and went into the station.

It was a pity, though, that she hadn't had a chance to explain. He had probably written her off as neurotic.

Stourwell City Hospital was a large modern building on the outskirts of the city, not far from the bypass. It was not an attractive place architecturally, but none of the people who worked there worried about that: it was functional, and that was all that mattered.

Simon spent some time discussing cases with his boss and then visited two emergency admissions. After that he ate his dinner in the canteen, where he was joined by his house physician, and the discussion began all over again. They drank their coffee in the doctors' common-room and Simon gave his junior instructions for the late round. That done, he was free to return to Hillside, though whether he would remain free was always an uncertain matter.

It was dusk when he drove through the gateway, and a crescent moon was clear and bright in the darkening sky above the park. Lights shone from the upper windows of the cottage and he knew that one or both of the sisters were at home. Suddenly feeling sociable, he called up the stairs as soon as he entered the house.

'Hi, girls! I'm just going to put the filter on. Want some coffee?'

Marie Evesham, tall and thin with mousy hair, appeared at the top of the stairs. She looked older than her thirty years, and her mother's illness had given her an underlying sadness which her friends sympathised with but could do nothing to alleviate.

'We were just going to make some, but yours always tastes better than ours.' She raised her voice. 'Are you coming down, Anna?'

The other sister joined her on the landing. 'I'd certainly like a chat *plus* coffee, of course. Lavinia says you've met Marie's replacement, and, since

I'll have to work with her, naturally I'm interested.'

They always referred to Miss Greenfield by her Christian name behind her back, but no one dared use it to her face.

'I've met a girl who's likely to be appointed, but it isn't official yet.' Simon went into his kitchen, leaving the door open so the conversation could be continued.

'Don't split hairs, Simon! You know perfectly well it's almost a cinch.' Anna Templeton, prettier and plumper than Marie, with dark curls tied back with a red ribbon, sat down on the sofa and pushed a cushion into the small of her back. 'What's her name?'

'Wendy something——' He paused to think. 'A Scottish name—oh, yes, I've got it. McBride.'

'How awful to be called Wendy!' Marie exclaimed. 'I bet people are always asking her where Peter Pan is.'

Simon reappeared in the doorway. 'It never entered my head. I merely thought how well the name suited her. Anyway, it wasn't her *name* that bothered me.'

Anna looked at him blankly. 'What on earth do you mean?'

'Well, for one thing she looks like a teenager.'

'Gosh! How old is she, then?'

'How should I know?'

'What's the other thing?' Marie wanted to know.

'I don't think she's very well, and her nerves are

in a shocking state. Lavinia asked me to drive her
to the station. I wasn't particularly pleased,
because I'd had to make a special trip out to
Hillside and I was in a hurry to get back to the
hospital——'

'It wasn't much of a detour, Simon,' Marie
pointed out.

'Granted. The fact is, I hadn't taken to the girl
and I didn't want to bother——'

'I suppose if she'd been a beautiful blonde you'd
have been only too eager?'

'Probably.' He grinned and disappeared again to
pour the coffee, re-emerging with three mugs on a
battered tin tray.

'You still haven't produced any evidence con-
cerning the state of her nerves,' Anna reminded
him, accepting her share of the strong black coffee.

'I'm coming to that. On the way to the station
we had a near-miss—nothing I couldn't handle—
and Wendy was so scared I thought she was going
to faint.'

'Oh, dear, that really *is* rather worrying. I do
hope she isn't as ineffectual as she sounds.' Marie
put down her mug and looked at him anxiously. 'I
was so hoping I'd be able to hand over to someone
I felt happy about, and this girl sounds quite
unsuitable. What on earth has come over Lavinia?'
Simon sipped his coffee thoughtfully. He had
asked himself that question as he drove away from
the station, but he had forgotten all about Wendy
McBride while his mind was fully occupied with

events at the hospital. A picture of her face looking at him through the car window as she thanked him for the lift floated before his inner vision. She would be quite pretty if she were not so pale, and the brief smile she had given him had quite transformed her.

'Well, of course, Lavinia presumably knows a lot more about her than we do,' he said judicially in answer to Anna's question. 'I suppose they must have spent a couple of hours together, but we're only judging by appearances.'

'Maybe we'd better reserve judgement?' Marie suggested. A shadow crossed her face and she added hastily, 'I meant you two had better keep an open mind. I don't expect I shall ever meet my successor.'

Simon and Anna exchanged glances, and by mutual consent the subject of Wendy McBride was shelved.

CHAPTER TWO

WENDY'S appointment to the post of sister at Hillside went without a hitch, but the waiting period, although it was short, she found traumatic. Her mother disapproved of her starting work so soon after the crash and enquired several times a day why she couldn't have given herself a longer period for convalescence.

'You'll probably find the post is too much for you and have to give it up,' she prophesied pessimistically. 'I noticed you were limping slightly this morning when you came back from the shops.'

'Only because I was tired.'

Barbara McBride pounced on the admission. 'You'll often be tired at that place.' She attacked a slab of pastry angrily with a rolling pin. 'And why on earth are you going so far away from home? Surely you could have got your old job back at the hospital here?'

'For heaven's sake!' Wendy exploded. 'It's only fifty miles——'

'It's a long way compared with being so close that you're able to live at home. Your gran and I are going to miss you coming in and out of the house most dreadfully.'

If Barbara had wanted to make her daughter feel

guilty, she was certainly succeeding, even though Wendy knew perfectly well she had committed no crime by wanting to have a change.

'I'm sorry, Mum,' she said impatiently, 'but it's done now, and I'm not going to back out now they've offered me the job officially. Couldn't you try and understand that I really do need to re-organise my life?'

Barbara sighed and shook her unnaturally dark head. 'I would have thought you'd want to be close to your nearest and dearest at a time like this—not running away from them.'

Wendy made no attempt to explain that she found the atmosphere at home claustrophobic. She didn't want to be fussed over and wrapped around by too much tender, loving care, particularly as she suspected some of it was due to an inability to accept that she was grown up.

She had been conscious of a desire for some-thing different even before she met Vernon. Then she had embarked on a whirlwind romance and thought no more about changing her job because she would be leaving home anyway—to get married.

But the accident on the motorway had changed all that, and made the need for a new life all the greater.

When the day on which it was to start came at last and she stood in the hall, waiting for the taxi, Barbara was still insisting that she wasn't fit to start work. Only her grandmother made an effort to see her off with a smile.

'You're a sensible girl—I'm sure you wouldn't take on something you couldn't manage.' She kissed Wendy affectionately as a car drew up outside. 'We're going to miss having a young person in the house, dear, but I expect you'll get a free weekend quite often and then you'll be able to come and see us. Take care of yourself.'

Barbara pulled herself together and echoed her mother's hopes. Bombarded by good wishes and last-minute regrets, Wendy went down the garden path and got into the taxi.

Her new life had begun, and she ought to be looking eagerly forward to the future. Instead she felt only a mild sense of release.

Perhaps it was too soon to be experiencing pleasurable anticipation? Maybe her mental recovery wasn't as far advanced as she had hoped?

Only last night she had had one of those awful nightmares which had haunted her ever since the crash. She was driving up the motorway in a tiny car no bigger than a tin box, and a monster vehicle had come hurtling through the air, straight towards her. She had awakened drenched in sweat and with a scream dying on her lips, and it had taken her a long time to get to sleep again. In the morning she had felt heavy-eyed and unrefreshed, and strangely reluctant to face the ordeals that lay ahead.

It was a relief to find her spirits rising as the

miles slipped by, and at Stourwell station she had
a pleasant surprise when she found Miss Greenfield
waiting to welcome her.

'I'll take you straight to the cottage,' the nursing
officer said as they left the car park. 'You'll be
anxious to get settled in. We're not, of course,
expecting you to go on duty today, but I hope
you'll come up to the house at lunchtime and meet
some of the people you're going to work with.'

'I'm longing to see my flatlet,' Wendy told her.
'I've never had a place of my own before.'

Miss Greenfield made no comment, but Wendy
sensed her slight surprise and wished she had not
made the confession. To admit she had lived at
home all her life—except during her first year as a
student nurse—would not at all help the mature
image she was struggling to maintain.

At the cottage a key was thrust into her hand
and she was abandoned, with her luggage, in a
tiny square hall. Feeling distinctly burglarish, she
climbed the stairs and came to a small landing
with two doors, one on either side.

As she stood wondering which door to try first,
a car drew up outside with a rattle of gravel. A
door slammed and footsteps came briskly up the
garden path. The front door opened and then shut
with a slam.

Peeping down over the banisters, Wendy saw a
reddish-brown head and broad shoulders in a
tweed jacket, and at that moment Simon Meadows

stumbled over the pile of luggage and said a loud and hearty 'Damn!'

'I'm so sorry,' Wendy apologised. 'I wouldn't have left it there if I'd known someone was coming.'

Of all the idiotic things to say!

She was not surprised when he retorted, 'Unless you're psychic I don't see how you could possibly have known. I suppose you're the new sister?'

'Yes, of course. We met when I came for my interview. You gave me a lift to the station.'

'So I did. It slipped my mind for the moment.' He bent and picked up the largest suitcase. 'I'll bring this up for you.'

In two or three bounds, so it seemed, he arrived on the landing and towered over her. She thanked him a little breathlessly and asked which was her flat.

'The one on your left. Anna Templeton occupies the other one, but I expect she's on duty. Marie—the sister you're replacing—left yesterday, so Anna will be busy.' He went leaping down the stairs again and had transferred everything to the landing by the time Wendy had unlocked her door, after which he disappeared into his own domain.

Wendy stood in the doorway and looked into her new home, and for the first time she felt a stirring of real excitement.

The bed-sitting-room was large and overlooked the park. It was furnished with several comfortable chairs and a bed disguised as a sofa. The colour scheme was a cool green and white, with bright splashes of apricot, and the paintwork looked fresh and clean. Two doors led respectively to a tiny shower-room and an equally small kitchen.

Wendy was delighted with it. She wandered round, taking it all in, and then plugged in the kettle.

Perhaps Simon would like some coffee, but when she called down the stairs to ask she found him on his way out. He had changed into a vivid green tracksuit and was wearing running shoes.

'Coffee? No, thanks, I had some at the hospital, and I'm off now for a run round the park. There's just time before lunch, which I'm going to eat at Hillside, because their food is much better than we get in Stourwell.' He paused with his hand on the knob of the front door. 'And if you're wondering how a hard-working registrar can go jogging in the middle of the day, I'd have you know this is supposed to be my *free* day, but I got tied up at the hospital and couldn't get away.'

The kettle was boiling, and Wendy made her coffee. She drank it at the window, gazing at the view and thinking how wonderfully rural and peaceful it looked, as unlike the busy—and ugly—town of Benham as anything could possibly be.

She'd done the right thing in applying for this job, she felt sure. Away from the stress and strain of a big hospital, and the frequent frustrations of home life, she would rapidly regain her normal health and strength, and put the horror of the accident behind her.

Half an hour later the flatlet had lost some of its tidiness and was beginning to look as though someone lived there. Wendy had not been able to carry anything heavy, but she had brought a few favourite ornaments and some paperbacks. Luckily there was already a good supply of cushions, and Marie had left behind several attractive pot plants.

She was standing in the middle of the room, admiring the results of her labours, when she heard the front door open again. This time light footsteps came up the stairs and there was a tap on her door. When she opened it she found a pretty dark girl standing there, wearing a sister's navy blue dress and with a lace-trimmed cap perched on her curls. She had a slight air of maturity and could have been any age between twenty-five and thirty-five.

'Hi, Wendy!' She smiled and advanced into the room. 'I'm Anna Templeton, and I've come to escort you to lunch at the house.'

'That's very nice of you,' Wendy said gratefully. 'Ought I to put on uniform?'

'There's no need, since you don't start until tomorrow. Just come as you are.'

Wendy glanced dubiously at her fawn cord trousers and yellow polo shirt. She would so much have preferred to meet the rest of the staff clad in appropriate clothes—it would have boosted her morale considerably—but it would look ridiculous to insist on getting into her uniform. There wasn't time to screw up her hair either.

'Just give me a minute to tidy myself,' she said, 'and I'll be with you.'

As she looked at herself in the mirror she saw that excitement had given her a wild rose colour which made her look quite different from the pale girl who had applied for the job and caused so much concern. She *was* much stronger than she had been then, and now that she had reached this stage she hoped every day would see an improvement.

As the two girls walked up the drive they caught a glimpse of a bright green figure speeding across a clearing in the distance.

'There goes Simon Meadows,' said Anna. 'I think you met him when you came for your interview, didn't you?'

'Miss Greenfield persuaded him to give me a lift to the station.' Wendy smiled wryly. 'I don't think he thought much of the idea.' She hesitated, then added, 'I couldn't help feeling he didn't at all approve of me as a prospective sister for Hillside.'

'He did seem to think you looked a bit frail,' Anna admitted, 'but you don't have to take any notice of that. He's so disgustingly healthy himself he tends to look down on lesser mortals.'

In spite of the encouraging words, she had sounded just slightly embarrassed, and Wendy guessed that Simon had probably given an unflattering description of herself. Sharing a house with the two sisters must mean he knew them quite well.

'I'm not quite up to my usual standard of fitness,' she confided, 'but I soon shall be.' She gave a brief account of the accident, not mentioning Vernon. 'You mustn't imagine I shan't be able to pull my weight, because I'm not anticipating any trouble at all.'

'Please don't feel you've got to prove yourself by taking up jogging or something daft like that,' Anna warned with a smile.

Wendy burst out laughing. 'There's no fear of that! It's never appealed to me anyway. Apart from swimming, I'm not very athletic.'

'Did you know we've got a pool here?'

'Miss Greenfield mentioned it, but I didn't see it.'

'It's in a separate building overlooking what used to be the stable yard—the gift of a grateful patient who inherited a lot of money shortly after he'd convalesced here. We all thought it was a super idea,' said Anna.

They rounded a curve in the drive and the house appeared before them in all its Georgian beauty. Anna led the way through the crowded hall to the dining-room, where a queue of patients was waiting for the gong. They stared at the stranger with idle curiosity, and Wendy was glad that her guide went straight into the dining-room where a long table by the window was apparently reserved for the staff. Two girls in primrose overalls were already there. One of them was the redhead Wendy remembered seeing on her previous visit, and Anna introduced her as Debra Jordan.

She seemed to be excited about something, and the other girl, who was brown-haired and called Jane Maxwell, was trying to keep her quiet.

'I tell you I saw him,' Debra insisted after casually acknowledging the introduction. 'He was jogging round the park, and that probably means he'll come here for lunch.'

'So what? He can eat sandwiches in the park or lunch at the Ritz for all I care. Do shut up about him!'

It was not hard to guess who was the object of Debra's interest, and Wendy repressed a tolerant smile. Simon Meadows, she supposed, was just the sort of macho male to attract a lively girl like this one, even though he must be at least ten years older.

The gong had sounded and the dining-room was filling up. Two middle-aged nurses in green uniforms joined them and one of them sat down next to Wendy, greeting her with a friendly 'Hello!'

'Just visiting, are you, dear?' she enquired after a moment.

'Oh, no—I'm going to work here——' Wendy broke off as Anna leaned forward.

'This is our new sister, Stella. Wendy McBride.'

To Wendy she added, 'Nurse Johnson is one of the stalwarts of Hillside. She's been here for ever.'

'Not quite, dear, but sometimes it feels like it.' Stella gave a comfortable chuckle which sounded as though she would allow very little to disturb her.

Nevertheless, Wendy had been conscious of a tiny pause, and she knew Nurse Johnson had been taken aback at this first sight of the new sister. If only she hadn't been wearing her hair in a ponytail. . .

Summoning all her composure, she embarked on a conventional exchange of remarks with her neighbour, and she was in the midst of saying how much she admired Hillside, both house and park, when she became aware of a sort of flutter opposite.

Simon, still wearing his tracksuit, had breezed into the room, causing Debra to snatch up the cardigan she had earlier placed on the empty chair next to her. The staff table was nearly full now and it seemed quite natural for him to take the seat beside her. Wendy smiled to herself. She could remember feeling like that about a good-looking young medic when she was in her first year as a student nurse. It hadn't lasted very long, and she hoped Debra's infatuation wouldn't either.

As she continued her conversation with Stella Johnson, she observed the two people opposite. Debra was talking eagerly and Simon was listening with flattering attention and a half-smile, no doubt thoroughly enjoying being adored by an attractive young girl.

Miss Greenfield came in, rather late, and inter-rupted their conversation with some brusqueness.

'I hope you remembered to take Mary Grieve's lunch tray up to her room, Debra?'

'Oh, yes, Miss Greenfield,' the girl assured her glibly.

'How did she receive it?'

'Well, I dunno, really. It didn't look as if she was very interested. I mean, she seemed half asleep, but I put it on the bed-table and helped her to sit up.'

'You'd better go up as soon as you've finished your own lunch and see how she's getting on.'

'Yes, Miss Greenfield.' With obvious relief, Debra returned her attention to Simon.

'Why is the lady having to eat in bed?' asked Wendy, turning towards Anna. 'I thought a con-valescent home didn't have bed patients.'

'We have to sometimes, but Mary isn't in bed because she's ill—at least, not exactly. She's had a mastectomy and seems quite unable to come to terms with it, and if she decides she isn't going to get up nobody seems able to shift her.'

'Would counselling help?'

'She's had some, but so far to no avail.' Anna paused to hand her empty plate to a waitress. 'At least we know where she is when she's in bed. The first day or two she was here she was con-

stantly disappearing into the park, and as she
never put a coat on it was very worrying.'

Wendy accepted a helping of apple tart and ice-
cream and wondered what to do with her afternoon. Outside the sun was shining and the park
beckoned her. She longed to go for a walk and do
some exploring, but she knew her ankle would
start aching if she overdid things, so she decided
to limit herself to a gentle stroll near the house.
She might go and peep into the greenhouses, or
perhaps walk round the lake she had glimpsed
away to the left.

'What are you going to do this afternoon?' asked
Anna as they left the dining-room.

Glad she had got it all worked out, Wendy said
she was going exploring, and was directed to
follow the corridor leading past Miss Greenfield's
office which would take her out via the stable yard.

'Don't forget to take a look at the swimming-
pool,' Anna called after her.

It would have been difficult to ignore it, as the
big building dominated the yard. All one side of it
was glass, and Wendy went close to it and peered
in, admiring the profusion of green plants and the
comfortable white-painted chairs. The blue water
rippled enticingly and she longed to dive in,
resolving to do so at the first opportunity.

She was about to start her walk when her eye
was caught by a movement on the other side of
the pool. Someone had opened a door and then
shut it quickly, apparently on seeing her. Perhaps

a patient was contemplating a dip and didn't want an onlooker? It seemed a strange time, just after lunch, but Wendy didn't feel sufficiently involved to regard it as any of her business, and she turned her back and strolled on.

A moment later her detached attitude received a severe jolt.

Rounding the corner of the building, she again glimpsed a movement out of the corner of her eye, and this time she turned her head in time to see a woman running at a good speed towards the nearest clump of rhododendrons. She was wearing a bright pink nightdress.

Wendy halted in dismay. No one should be running around in a public park clad only in her nightwear. She supposed the obvious thing was to set off in pursuit, but it seemed unlikely she would catch the fugitive in her present slightly handi-capped state. Far better to hurry back to the house and report what she had seen.

When she arrived breathless in the back corridor she found herself in the middle of a scene. Debra stood at the bottom of a narrow flight of stairs waving her hands about and exclaiming excitedly, 'She hasn't even eaten her lunch, Miss Greenfield, and she isn't in the toilet or anywhere upstairs——'

Although she was addressing the sister-in-charge, she also had a fascinated audience of kitchen staff and, in the background, Simon Meadows stood listening intently.

'How very tiresome!'

Miss Greenfield was refusing to show alarm, but Wendy guessed she must be worried, and she squeezed her way through to the centre of the group.

'Excuse me—are you talking about a patient in a pink nightdress?' she asked.

'Yes—Mary Grieve. Have you seen her?'

'It was the merest glimpse, but she ran away when she saw me—I didn't know who it was, of course, but——'

'It seems highly probable that it was Mary. Couldn't you have called out to her, or at least done *something* to stop her?'

'I didn't think I stood much chance—after all, she didn't know me——'

'Well, never mind now. The important thing is to organise a search party as quickly as possible.'

'Oh, please, Miss Greenfield,' Debra burst out, 'can I go?'

'I think you'd better be one of them, and Sister McBride will go with you and indicate the spot where she last saw Mary.'

Simon had moved quietly forward and now stood in their midst, towering over everybody. 'I'll come as well,' he said decisively. 'They may need help.'

'It's very good of you, Dr Meadows, but I hardly like to put you to the trouble on your day off——'

'It's no trouble at all.'

'Well, I'm sure both Sister and Debra would be glad of your assistance.'

Wendy's eyes alighted for a moment on the girl's face, and it was easy to see she could scarcely conceal her pleasure. No doubt she would like the search prolonged as much as possible, whereas in her own case she was hoping it would be very short indeed. If she had to spend much time hunting the missing patient, how on earth could she possibly conceal from her fellow searchers that she wasn't up to that sort of activity?

'Where did you see Mary?' Simon demanded as they crossed the yard.

Wendy thought rapidly. There were so many clumps of rhododendrons—how could she be sure of indicating the right one? Fortunately at that moment they passed the end of the swimming-pool and her visual memory prodded her into showing them the exact spot.

'Surely she's not likely to be there now?' Debra protested.

'No, but we've got to start somewhere.' He lengthened his stride, and the teenager skipped along effortlessly at his side.

No one seemed to notice that Wendy had difficulty in keeping up.

They reached the tall, wide-spreading bushes and searched among them, just in case the fugitive was hiding, but without result. From that position quite a wide expanse of the park could be seen, and Simon decreed that they should make their

way towards a distant clump of trees, keeping a
keen lookout for a flash of bright pink.

Until that moment Wendy had not realised that
Hillside was well named. The ground now sloped
steadily upward and she found it harder than ever
to stand the pace. Already her ankle was aching,
and she wondered what would happen if she had
to do any running.

She soon found out.

CHAPTER THREE

'THERE she is!' Debra's voice rose excitedly, and Simon clapped his hand over her mouth.

'S-sh! We don't want her to hear us.'

They had worked their way cautiously through the trees and were about to emerge on the other side when Debra, who was leading, made her discovery. A moment later they all saw the figure sitting on a seat with her back turned about a hundred yards away. She had reached the highest point of the little hill and was apparently staring out over open country.

Simon rapidly took charge of the situation, and, in the midst of her concern both for the distressed patient and herself, Wendy found a moment in which to criticise his assumption of authority. Why, just because he was a man, should he automatically take it for granted he knew best?

'It's obviously impossible to get right up to the seat without Mary sensing we're behind her, even if we don't make a sound, so we must fan out and approach from three different directions. Then, as soon as she becomes aware of us and takes off, one of us will be strategically placed to intercept her.'

Oh no, prayed Wendy, don't let it be me!

They parted and began their stealthy approach. Concentrating on the route allotted to her, Wendy saw a small bush ahead and decided to shelter there momentarily in order to reconnoitre. When she reached it she checked on the position of the other two and found they were within a few yards of the seat.

It was just then that some sixth sense warned Mary Grieve of danger behind her. She leapt to her feet and began to run in what seemed to her to be the best direction. Straight towards the bush where Wendy still lingered.

Frantic thoughts raced through Wendy's mind. She felt quite incapable of a physical attack, but perhaps, since she was a stranger and not in uniform, she might try to hold the fugitive in casual talk until the others got there. Accordingly, she stepped out right into Mary's path and said a friendly, 'Hello! Isn't it a lovely day?'

To her horror Mary flung her a terrified glance and veered sharply off in a different direction. She heard Simon shout, 'Stop her!' and valiantly tried to obey. But the quarry was already well out of reach, and although Wendy began to run as fast as she could, it was obvious she had no hope of catching her.

As she panted in pursuit Simon flashed past her, followed closely by Debra, and she saw them draw level, one on either side, and each take one of Mary's arms. There was a brief struggle, and

then the distraught patient suddenly gave in and
burst into tears.

As Debra stood helpless, quite unable to cope
with adult tears, Simon put his arm round the
sobbing woman and drew her close, stroking her
lank black hair with his free hand and murmuring
words of comfort. And suddenly Wendy forgot
about her ankle and once more remembered she
was a nurse instead of an unwilling athlete. Pulling
off her anorak, she put it round Mary's shoulders
and took her gently by the arm.

'You'll get pneumonia if we stay out here any
longer,' she said quietly. 'Let's go back to the
house and get someone to make a nice hot cup of
tea for you. As a matter of fact, I could do with
one myself.'

'Me too,' Simon put in cheerfully.

They began to walk back slowly, the runaway
held firmly but not too tightly between them,
while Debra followed disconsolately behind, kicking at the dead leaves left by the previous autumn.

It seemed a long way to the house and Wendy's
ankle was protesting vigorously by the time they
got there, so that she found it impossible not to
limp, though she tried to do it unobtrusively.

Miss Greenfield met them in the back corridor,
her relief hidden behind a welcoming smile.

'I'm so sorry you got let in for this before you'd
even started work here,' she said to Wendy in a
low voice. 'I assure you it doesn't happen very
often.'

Wendy smiled and murmured something appropriate. With all her heart she hoped it didn't.

When the others had disappeared upstairs, she debated what to do with what remained of the afternoon. She had already explored rather more of the park than she had intended, and the lure of her pleasant little flat was getting stronger by the minute. She would go straight back, she decided, and make a pot of tea, and after that she might finish her unpacking if she felt up to it.

As she set forth she remembered that Mary still had her anorak, but she wasn't cold after so much exercise, so she decided not to bother with going back for it. She could easily pick it up in the morning.

But she didn't have to wait that long.

She was sipping her tea gratefully, and resting her ankle in a comfortable chair, when the doorbell rang.

'You forgot your anorak,' said Simon, holding it out to her.

'I didn't exactly forget it.' Wendy took it from him. 'I decided it would do quite well in the morning.'

'There's gratitude for you!' he said lightly.

She laughed and apologised. 'Would you like a cup of tea as a reward? I've just made some.'

He accepted at once and looked round with interest as he entered the flat. 'You've made it look quite lived in already,' he remarked.

'It's wonderful what a few books and ornaments

will do.' She handed him a cup and he sat down in the armchair opposite, settling himself comfortably and looking thoroughly at home.

Very probably he was. No doubt there was quite a lot of socialising between the two nurses and the doctor living at the cottage. At that moment the thought crossed her mind that she had only been there half a day and she had already offered Simon coffee—which he had refused—and now tea. With all her heart she hoped he would realise the two invitations were due to good manners and nothing else.

'How was Mary when you left the house?' she asked.

'Already responding to the sedation I ordered for her.' He sighed and briefly let his perplexity show. 'But I'm only too well aware—as I'm sure you are too—that sedation isn't the answer. She's got to be helped to come to terms with the loss of a breast, but I feel completely out of my depth, because a bloke hasn't the faintest chance of understanding how a woman feels under those circumstances.'

'I don't think anybody does who hasn't experienced it,' Wendy said thoughtfully. 'I suppose it must be awful, knowing a vital part of your femininity has been removed and you'll never get it back. Women who've had a hysterectomy sometimes suffer similarly, particularly if they're on the young side.'

They were silent for a moment, brooding on the

problem of Mary Grieve, then Simon abruptly changed the subject.

'Does your ankle feel better now?'

'My ankle?' She was completely taken aback.

'I noticed you were limping.'

'Oh, dear—I hoped it didn't show.' Wendy hesitated and then went on, 'I was in a car crash not long ago and my ankle was badly sprained. I don't expect it will bother me at all while I'm working at the house, but I didn't bargain for having to run races in the park!'

'A bad sprain sometimes takes longer to mend than a fracture,' said Simon. 'It would be a good idea to rest it as much as possible when you're off duty——'

'I know that!' He raised his eyebrows and Wendy said hastily, 'Sorry! It's just that I didn't want anybody to know about it and I'm annoyed because it's been discovered before I've even started work.'

'No one would have noticed if it hadn't been for this afternoon's chase, and I'm almost certainly the only one who knows. Debra's a dear child, but quite unobservant of anything that doesn't interest her.'

'She'll have to do better than that when she starts nursing seriously.'

'She'll be older then and more responsible.' Simon glanced at his watch. 'I'd better go and have a shower—I've got a theatre date in the city this evening. I suppose you've heard of our famous Regency Theatre?'

'I think so,' Wendy said cautiously, 'but I've never been there.'

He rose to his feet in one lithe movement. 'You must go at the first opportunity. It's unique—well, very nearly. I believe there are one or two others that have survived from the early nineteenth century.' At the door he waved a nonchalant hand. 'Thanks for the tea. Be seeing you!'

He left Wendy feeling slightly wistful. Not so very long ago her life had been full of dates, and now that she had recovered most of her strength after the accident she had begun to miss them. Yet, at the same time, she didn't really feel ready to start on a grand rebuilding programme.

Tired out after the eventful day, she went early to bed and soon fell asleep in spite of the unfamiliar silence which was wrapped like a blanket round the cottage.

The sound of a car awakened her and a moment later she heard the front door shut softly. Curiosity made her switch on the light and look at her little travelling clock. It was two a.m.

It must have been a very enjoyable date for Simon to prolong it to such an extent!

The park was deserted as Anna and Wendy walked up the drive the following morning. Both wore navy cardigans over their uniforms and carried their lace-trimmed caps; both also wore their hair in ponytails.

Wendy had come out of her flat with her hair in its tight topknot and had been the recipient of a startled stare from Anna.

'I hardly recognised you,' the other sister said frankly. 'Do you always wear your hair like that when you're on duty?'

'Only when I want to look older than I am.'

'It certainly makes you look severe.' Anna hesitated, evidently uncertain of how far she could go in personal criticism. 'Your hair's such a pretty colour—like ripe corn. I'm sure the patients would like to see more of it, and I wouldn't be surprised if they'd like to see you looking young too. After all, you're fully qualified.'

With scarcely a moment's hesitation, Wendy had turned back, dragged out the pins and substituted a scrap of white ribbon. Her reflection looked at her from the mirror, familiar and friendly, and once more apparently not a day more than twenty.

She'd got the job, and she didn't have to pretend. All she had to do now was prove herself, and that she was quite determined to accomplish.

'I wonder how Mary Grieve is this morning,' she said as the house came in sight.

Anna's round cheerful face wore a troubled expression. 'I wish I could tell you I believe she may be more resigned, but it wouldn't be true. It seems to me she's got a very long way to go before she reaches that stage.'

'What will happen to her? Will she stay here?'

'They don't like keeping people more than two weeks, but it does happen sometimes. A lot depends on the home circumstances, and I think Mary lives alone in a bed-sitting-room. That wouldn't be at all a suitable background for her just now.'

'It certainly wouldn't help her depression.'

Wendy's thoughts flew to her own home background. Had she perhaps been ungrateful in not appreciating the fussing she had received? She had often longed to be by herself, not to have to make a suitable response when her mother kept on about her health and the importance of eating nourishing food, and not being in too much of a hurry to get going again—when all she had wanted was to be left alone.

Maybe if Mary had had some of that sort of treatment she would not be in such a state now. Wendy had, of course, called her mother when she had arrived, but she reflected now that she must go and see her when she got the chance.

'The first job,' Anna said as they entered by the main door, 'is the morning medicine round. Marie and I usually went round together if we were both on duty, largely to give us both a chance of checking on each patient at the beginning of the day.'

'The night nurse doesn't do it? Give out the medicines, I mean.'

'She's too busy, and she couldn't do it alone

because there's no one to check her except Lavinia, and she wouldn't want to be bothered so early. You and I don't need checking, of course, except in a few cases where there's a really dangerous drug being given.'

'Surely you don't have many of those!'

'Oh, no, but we occasionally have someone on morphine——'

'In a convalescent home?' queried Wendy.

Anna lowered her voice. 'We have a single room which is kept for terminally ill patients who'd go to a hospice if there was one in Stourwell. We keep them for a short time and then they're returned to hospital for the last stage.'

Wendy allowed her astonishment to show. 'I would never have expected to find a case of that sort at Hillside. What do the other patients think about it?'

'I doubt if they know. Usually the person concerned is too ill to get up.' Anna sighed and then added, 'It was awful for Marie after she knew her mother was in the same state.'

Wendy digested the information in silence, then pushed it to the back of her mind as they went to the cloakroom to put on their caps. As she anchored her sister's cap securely in place with white hairgrips, she was conscious of a surge of pride mixed with a feeling of unreality. It was strange to reflect that her present eminence was entirely due to the accident.

Anna disappeared into the office to get the keys

of the drugs cupboard and then they went upstairs together. The patients were mostly beginning to dress, though some of the men clung to their bedclothes and feigned sleep. Anna dealt cheerfully but ruthlessly with them, and soon everyone except Mary Grieve was well on the way towards being ready for breakfast.

The mastectomy case was still under sedation, and Anna decided to allow her to remain in bed.

'At least we'll know where she is,' she murmured to Wendy.

'We didn't yesterday.'

'She wasn't drugged then.'

Miss Greenfield did not appear until they all went into breakfast. Wendy was conscious of a close scrutiny, but no mention was made of her hairstyle. Instead she was asked whether Anna had told her about morning surgery.

'We were talking non-stop all the way here,' Anna laughed, 'but somehow we didn't get around to it.'

The nursing officer raised her eyebrows slightly but made no comment. Briskly and efficiently, she put Wendy in the picture.

'We have an arrangement whereby patients with problems—real or imaginary—can consult a sister between the hours of nine-thirty and eleven o'clock in the surgery on the first floor. Normally you will take it in turns to be in charge, but today I'd like you to work together. It will help you to get to know the patients.'

When, later on, they went along to the surgery they found a line of patients already waiting on chairs in the corridor. They all looked with interest at the new sister, and Wendy tried not to imagine their comments.

'Do we get many customers?' she asked as she took her place beside Anna at the desk.

'You'd be surprised! Of course, most of the things they consult us about are routine—indigestion, constipation and sleeping problems—but occasionally we pick up a warning of something more serious.'

'Like what?'

'Well, once we had a woman who'd been in hospital with viral pneumonia and she was sent here to recuperate because her husband was an invalid and couldn't look after her. She'd only been here two days when her appendix blew up. It was discovered when she came to surgery looking ghastly and complaining of abdominal pain.'

There were no startling cases that morning and they had finished long before eleven o'clock. Drinking coffee with Miss Greenfield in her sitting-room, they discussed the cases they had seen and then touched briefly on the subject of Mary Grieve.

'Her social worker is coming to see her today,' the sister-in-charge told them. 'I don't know if it will do any good, but we can only hope. In the meantime, she's to remain mildly sedated.'

Anna was off duty in the afternoon and Wendy spent her time trying to get to know the patients.

As there were fifty of them she did not feel she made much progress, but at least she managed to learn some of the names. By the time Anna returned and it was her own turn to go off, she was beginning to be conscious of an aching ankle and a brain bursting with a long list of varied complaints, only a few of which could be matched to the right names.

There was no one about when she went down the drive, so she could allow herself to limp, which made walking much easier. As she unlocked the front door of the cottage, she thought pleasurably of the long, lazy evening ahead.

It might be a lonely one, but she wouldn't mind that. It was still very much a novelty to be mistress of her own domain and accountable to no one.

The loneliness lasted only until nine o'clock.

Wendy had cooked herself an omelette and eaten it on her lap before the television, after which she had a hot shower and put on a blue velour caftan. She was watching the news when she heard someone at the door.

It couldn't be Anna, because she had gone to see her parents, who lived in the city. Her heart beating a little faster than usual—though she couldn't think why—Wendy opened the door and admitted Simon.

'What a transformation!' He looked her up and down appreciatively. 'You ought to wear your hair loose more often. I like it a lot better than that prim little knob you wore on top of your head when we first met. I'm sure you're not really prim.' He hesitated, then added with a twinkle, 'Well, fairly sure!'

She laughed and felt herself colouring, but she did not take up the challenge he had offered her. Switching off the television, she asked, 'Is this just a social call? Or did you think there might be some coffee available?'

'You make me sound as though I'm always on the scrounge.'

'I didn't mean to. I haven't known you long enough for that.'

'After all that chasing about in the park yesterday, I feel we've known each other much longer than is actually the case. Don't you?'

The only possible answer to that was a shrug, after which they were silent for a moment. Then Simon suddenly dropped his light, slightly teasing manner.

'As a matter of fact, I called to ask about Mary Grieve. How is she today?'

'Quiet, but obviously very depressed. She had some counselling this afternoon, but I don't know if it did any good.'

'We can only keep on trying. She isn't bad enough for real psychiatric treatment, not even when she ran into the park in her nightie.'

'Could be she had an attack of claustrophobia,' Wendy said thoughtfully. 'I know the feeling——'

Simon looked at her in surprise. 'You suffer from claustrophobia?'

'Not in the ordinary sense.' She was annoyed with herself for giving that much away. 'I mean, I don't mind being in a crowded lift or a packed tube train, but I know what it feels like to want to get away from—people.'

There was a pause, then he asked, 'Would you care to enlarge on that?'

'No, thanks.'

He raised strongly marked eyebrows. 'Another time, perhaps?'

'Maybe,' Wendy surprised herself by saying.

This time Simon made no attempt to break the silence, but to Wendy it seemed increasingly uncomfortable. The quiet outside world offered nothing worthy of comment. The children who played in the park after tea had long since gone home and the birds had retired to rest. Owls were calling in the trees behind the big house, but their eerie cries scarcely impinged on the still room. She could hear Simon breathing and had a horrible feeling that her own breaths were quickening.

'I do wish you'd have some coffee——' She was up on her feet.

He raised his hand to stop her. 'If you happen to have any beer, I wouldn't say no.'

'Sorry. I don't like it.'

'Pity. I've somehow managed to let myself run out, and I can't go out to get some at the local because I'm on call. One disadvantage of living out here is that I can't be bleeped, so I must stay near a phone.' He hesitated, then added with a grin, 'I suppose you wouldn't like to get dressed properly and go and get some for me? The pub's only just down the road.'

The effrontery of the man! 'No, I would not!' Wendy flung back at him. 'It's probably very good for you to have to do without—specially as you're on call.'

He sighed, but did not try to persuade her. 'I hadn't much hope that you'd agree to being errand girl, but it was worth a try.'

'I'm glad you're not too disappointed,' Wendy said acidly.

'How's your ankle?' was his next question.

'Aching a little, but I expect it will soon be quite all right again.' A sudden thought struck her. 'By the way, Miss Greenfield doesn't know I'm suffering a little from the effects of the accident, so I'd be obliged if you wouldn't mention it in front of her. Not that you're likely to, of course.'

Simon promised at once, then stood up with some reluctance. 'I'm sure you're longing to resume your peaceful evening, so I'll retreat to my flat. Be seeing you.'

At the door Wendy said politely, 'I hope you don't get a disturbed night.'

'If I do I'll try not to disturb *you*—and Anna.' He paused, his eyes raking her slight figure in the caftan. 'I must say you look very fetching in that blue garment. Quite irresistible, in fact.'

And before she could protest or move out of reach, he had put both hands on her shoulders, looked deep into her eyes and kissed her firmly on the lips.

Considerably shaken, Wendy shut the door quickly behind him and leaned back against it. No man had kissed her since Vernon died, and she was greatly taken aback at the strength of her emotions.

Surely she wasn't sex-starved already? Disgusted with herself, she switched on the television again and tried to concentrate on a discussion programme, but at the end of it she had no idea what the people involved had been talking about.

There was no denying that Simon was dominating her thoughts to an absurd degree—and not only her thoughts. She had only been at Hillside two days, but already he had visited her flat three times, though admittedly the first time he had only carried up her luggage. Added to that, she had shared the Mary Grieve episode with him, and they had also had an astonishing amount of rather personal conversation.

It just wouldn't do. She had no wish to get involved, however light-heartedly, with another man, and she had a strong suspicion that Simon was the sort who prided himself on his success with women. In future she would be very much on her guard—coolly friendly but no more.

The trouble was, for at least part of the time, she couldn't help liking him.

CHAPTER FOUR

WHEN Simon got back to his flat he felt strangely restless, and it was almost a relief when the telephone rang.

'Dr Meadows,' he said curtly.

'Staff Nurse Barber here,' said a soft voice, and he could hear that she was smiling. 'You sounded very formal, Simon!'

'I didn't know it was you, did I?'

'I suppose not. Anyway, this isn't a personal call. You're wanted urgently in A and E. We've got a case of cardiac arrest—a man who collapsed in a pub. The team managed to get him started again, but he's in a bad way, and both Sister and your house physician think you ought to see him. So will you come over pronto, please?'

'I'm on my way.'

Simon hung up the receiver, checked that his car keys were in his pocket and went outside, slamming the door behind him. As he started on the short drive to the City Hospital, he reflected that only a little while ago he would have been glad of the opportunity to see and talk to Helen Barber, even though both were on duty.

Now he was not so sure.

The expression 'not just a pretty face' flashed

into his mind and he knew his present perturbation was due to his suspicion that Helen *was* just
a pretty face, that behind those perfect features
and pale blonde hair there was a human being
singularly lacking in personality.

Brains she must have, or she wouldn't have
qualified and become a staff nurse, but it seemed
that many of the qualities which would make her
an interesting person were lacking, including a
sense of humour.

Braking sharply as a traffic light turned red, he
wondered what he should do about Helen. It was
embarrassing to be aware, when they were
together, that she was quite unconscious of the
change in him. Last night, for instance, after the
theatre, she had made it clear she was expecting a
lovemaking session in his car. He had definitely
not been in the mood, and it was difficult to
extricate himself without hurting her feelings. He
hoped he had managed it, but he could not be
sure.

Fortunately, now that she was on night duty in
A and E they had few opportunities for meeting,
and with any luck the situation would resolve
itself. He would just have to wait and see.

Simon's troubled thoughts ceased abruptly as he
swung into the hospital car park, and his professional self took over. Helen, equally formal, was
looking out for him, and she led him past a couple
of drunks, an old man apparently sound asleep,

and two women with a small, frightened girl between them, until they came to the first cubicle.

Ashen-faced, with sweat still shining on his brow, the patient scarcely seemed conscious. Sister stood beside him with her fingers on his wrist, and Helen took up her position in the background.

Simon asked a few questions, examined the man with great care, then stood looking down at him thoughtfully.

'Has his next of kin been informed?' he asked suddenly.

'We haven't been able to find out who they are,' Sister told him. 'Nobody came in with him, and there was nothing in his pockets except a handkerchief and a little money——'

'There was a front-door key,' Helen put in.

'Yes, but it's no use when we have no idea what it fits.'

Simon bent his head and sniffed. 'Could be this suit has just come back from the cleaners'—that would account for the empty pockets. Have you informed the police?'

'Not yet.' Well known for her fondness for sarcasm, Sister permitted herself an acid comment. 'We've been rather busy saving his life, Doctor, but Staff will go and attend to it now.'

Simon ignored the thrust. 'He's certainly in no state to be sent home—particularly as we don't know where that is. Have you been able to find a bed for him?'

'They're holding one in Henry Smithson Ward—

reluctantly, I might add—but I knew you'd want him hospitalised.'

He nodded and began to write on a prescription pad. 'Is there anything else you want me for while I'm here?' he asked when he had finished.

'Not at present, Doctor.'

Simon said goodnight, paused for a word with the Casualty Officer and left the department. As he pushed his way through the swing doors he realised that Helen was behind him.

'I rang the police,' she said breathlessly, 'but nobody had been reported missing.'

'It's only ten o'clock,' he pointed out. 'Much too soon for our chap. I suppose you gave a description of him as far as you could?'

'I did my best.' She slipped her arm into his as they walked towards his car. 'I did enjoy the theatre last night, Simon.'

'So did I.' Hastily he added, 'It was a very good play.'

An ambulance with its siren sounding swept up the drive and brought the stilted conversation to an end. As he drove away Simon wondered whether Helen had been aware of his lack of warmth, and concluded that she probably hadn't. She seemed to have no instinctive knowledge of a man's mind or mood, nor that he needed something more than mere physical pleasure.

He sighed and wondered if he was being unnecessarily solemn about the whole thing. Most men would be content to have Staff Nurse Helen

Barber as a girlfriend, so why could he not just accept her limitations and leave it at that?

Wendy heard his car return and wondered, with professional interest, what he had had to deal with at the hospital.

He was followed, a few minutes later, by another car which she presumed must be Anna's, and after that, as far as Wendy was aware, the silence of the park was unbroken.

She woke early and was pleased to find herself looking forward to her second day at Hillside, though she was a little nervous at the thought of taking surgery by herself. None of her experience as a staff nurse had prepared her for the role of family doctor, but it was comforting to know that her diagnostic skill would be unlikely to be severely tested.

And so it turned out, though she sensed that one or two of the patients were a little dubious of her youthful appearance. One of the elderly men, who was smartly turned out and wore a spotted bow tie, flirted with her outrageously, but she managed to handle him without giving offence.

There was one slightly disturbing incident. The line of chairs in the corridor had slowly emptied, and Wendy opened the door to make sure no one else was waiting. To her surprise she saw Mary Grieve sitting by herself at the far end.

'Did you want me?' she asked, smiling, when the patient made no attempt to approach.

'No!' Mary leapt to her feet and stood poised for flight. 'I—I was just sitting there—I don't want anybody——' And she rushed away down the corridor.

Wendy debated whether to follow her and decided against it, but she was a little uneasy about the incident and seized the first opportunity to tell Anna that Mary had apparently made an attempt to consult a sister on some matter and then taken fright.

'I'll look out for her tomorrow,' Anna promised, 'but I shan't be surprised if she doesn't turn up. She's keeping a very low profile at present and not allowing anyone to get a glimpse of her emotions. It's as though she'd closed right up like—like a sea anemone when you touch it.'

Wendy smiled at the simile but was immediately serious again. 'Perhaps she's making a real effort to come to terms with what's happened to her.'

'Or it could mean she's bottling everything up, and that can't be good for her, though it makes life easier for us.'

Mary did not reappear at surgery until nearly the end of Wendy's first week, and then, as before, she waited until all the other patients had been seen. But this time she did not run away.

'Come in, Mary.' Wendy produced what she hoped was a friendly smile. 'Is there something I can do for you?'

The patient, who had been hiding her left hand under her other arm, brought it out slowly and displayed the palm. It was red, swollen and obviously very painful.

'Whatever have you done to make it so inflamed?' Wendy asked in surprise.

'It's a splinter.' Mary swallowed nervously and her muddy brown eyes avoided Wendy's concerned gaze. 'I—I got it when I sat on that seat in the park, but it was a day or two before I took any notice of it.'

'By that time it must have been hurting quite a lot.'

'Yes, it was. I—I tried to get it out with a needle, but it had gone in too deep. I poked it about a bit and thought perhaps it might make its own way out.' And she added defiantly, 'Splinters do sometimes.'

'Very small ones can, but not slivers of wood like this one.' Wendy took the hand gently in both her own and studied the problem.

'I think I can move it without hurting you too much,' she said eventually, 'but you'll have to keep very still. Do you think you can manage that?'

Mary nodded, and she went to fetch surgical spirit and a probe. When the area all round the wound had been thoroughly cleaned, she explored it gently, all the while alert to any sudden movement from her patient. She heard Mary draw in a long quivering breath, but she kept still, and a moment later the splinter was out.

'Please keep your hand dry and try not to use

it.' Wendy applied a dressing and deftly bandaged it into place. 'I think you'd better attend surgery again tomorrow.'

'It won't be you, will it?'

'No, but Sister Templeton is very nice——'

'I'd rather see you. You were kind to me when I made a fool of myself by running away.'

Wendy was touched at the unexpected tribute. It would have been more natural if Mary had hated to be reminded of that day. An idea popped into her head, but she hesitated whether to act on it. Mary seemed more approachable than she had ever known her, but to reopen the subject of her operation might do more harm than good.

She decided to risk it.

'I can understand how you felt when you went rushing off into the park. It was because you wanted to get away from the house and everybody in it—isn't that right?'

'How do you know?' the patient demanded.

'I've felt like that too, but for an entirely different reason.' Wendy hesitated again. 'Do you mind if I ask whether you're now a little more resigned to what's happened?'

'Resigned?' To her surprise, Mary shrugged. 'If you're talking about losing a breast, I've been resigned ever since I got over the shock. I've never been very interested in men and I'm nearly thirty-nine, so I don't expect I'll change now. It doesn't seem so dreadful to me as it would to some women.'

Wendy gazed at her in total bewilderment. 'I don't understand. If you're so philosophical about having a mastectomy, why have you been working yourself up into such a state?' And giving us so much trouble, she added silently.

Mary sprang to her feet and took a few agitated steps about the surgery. 'Wouldn't *you* be in a state if you were told you'd got cancer?'

'Well, yes, I expect I would at first, but——'

'It's not just the breast—I'm sure to get it some-where else before long, and then I'll have to have more operations, and after a while they'll tell me I've got secondaries and they can't operate any more—and—and then I'll die——'

'Stop!'

Now, at last, Wendy understood. She got up from her chair and came round the desk to perch on the edge of it close to Mary. Leaning forward, she took the unbandaged hand into a firm clasp.

'Listen to me.' She made sure she held Mary's gaze and went on speaking slowly and clearly. 'I admit it's possible all your fears will materialise, *but it's most unlikely*. I've nursed patients who'd lost one or both breasts years ago, and they've been in hospital for entirely different reasons—nothing to do with cancer. My own mother has a friend who had a double mastectomy *twenty years* ago, and she's one of the healthiest women I know.'

She paused, but continued her steady gaze. 'So do you see you've been torturing yourself unnecessarily? I agree that you stand a chance of having the other breast removed, but that should be the end of it. Truly, I'm not making it all up just to stop you being so scared.'

There was dead silence in the surgery, and she had to struggle not to hold her breath as she waited for a reply. When it came at last it was spoken in a low, hesitant voice, but the words were reassuring.

'On your honour, you're not making it up?'

Inspiration suddenly came to Wendy. She smiled and said, 'Guide's honour.'

Mary actually smiled too. 'I used to be a Guide captain once. Perhaps I might go back to it. I believe they're always short of officers.'

'Sounds like a good idea.'

'I do feel so ashamed, though, making such a nuisance of myself. What must you all think of me?'

'We've all been so sorry we didn't seem able to help you,' Wendy told her. 'If only we'd known what the real trouble was—but everybody took it for granted you were upset because you felt— mutilated.'

'I suppose I did at first, as I said, but I soon got over it.' Mary raised her head in a challenging way. 'You probably think I'm lesbian because I don't care about men, but I'm not. I'm just not very interested in sex. Can you understand that?'

Wendy couldn't, but she kept it to herself. 'I expect there are lots of women who feel like that,

but you're obviously one of those who fully under-
stands her own nature and accepts it. Do you feel
better about the whole thing now?'

'Oh, yes—you've been a great help, and I'm
ever so grateful.'

It was obviously time to end the interview.
Wendy slid down from the desk and said briskly,
'You'll take care of that hand, won't you? I think
you should have a short course of antibiotics, but I
shall have to ask Dr Meadows to prescribe for
you.'

Alone at last, she sat brooding for a moment
before clearing up the surgery. It was difficult not
to feel triumphant because she had stumbled on
the real cause of the patient's behaviour, but she
knew it was largely a matter of luck.

As she left the surgery it occurred to her that
she ought to tell Miss Greenfield about her success, and also mention the poisoned hand. It was
pleasant to receive the nursing officer's congratu-
lations, and also to have her advice about the
splinter confirmed.

'The silly woman, keeping it to herself like
that. She might have got blood-poisoning.' Miss
Greenfield scribbled on a pad. 'Fortunately the
antibiotics should ward off any real trouble. I'll
tryand get Simon on the phone at once.'

'He says he'll come over at lunchtime,' she
reported a moment later. 'I didn't want to take up
his time by telling him about your success on the

psychological side, but I know he'll be very pleased.'

It was nearly two o'clock when Simon reached Hillside and Wendy was about to go off duty. He was in a hurry and made only a fleeting visit, escorted by Miss Greenfield, with the result that Wendy, sauntering down the drive, was overtaken by his car before she reached the cottage.

'I hear you've been covering yourself with glory.' He grinned at her through the open window.

'Not really. It was just luck.'

'Don't spoil it by false modesty.'

'It's *not* false!' She reacted immediately. 'The only thing I can take credit for is seizing the opportunity when Mary handed it to me on a plate.'

'Have it your own way. Seriously, though, I'd be interested to hear the details. Come down to the flat this evening and tell me all about it. Bring Anna with you if she's not doing anything special.'

He'd taken it for granted that *she* would be free, Wendy reflected, but couldn't really blame him. She had not had any social engagements since coming to Hillside.

'What time shall we come?' she asked.

'Goodness knows.' He shrugged. 'But you'll hear my car. Give me ten minutes and then turn up.' Morosely, he added, 'We've got problems at the hospital, so I might be late, but I'd still like a visit, if you think you can put up with a host who may not be in the best of tempers.'

Wendy looked after him dubiously as the car sped away. As an invitation it left a lot to be desired, but she found herself hoping he wouldn't be so late home that it wouldn't be worthwhile descending the stairs for coffee and conversation. Or whatever else he had to offer.

'I can't possibly go,' said Anna when the invitation was relayed to her. 'I promised my mother I'd go over and help her cut out a dress she wants to make for herself for my nephew's eighteenth birthday. She's a very good dressmaker, but she does hate cutting out.'

'How wonderfully involved with your family you are!' Wendy couldn't help exclaiming.

'How do you mean?'

'Well, you all seem to get on marvellously together.'

Anna laughed. 'Not all of us. My eldest brother is an absolute dead loss, but I suppose the rest of us rub along quite well. Of course, we're quite a big family, and that helps. I'm one of six and all of us married, so——'

'Are *you* married?' Wendy exclaimed in surprise.

'Didn't you know? Actually, I'm divorced, and I'm the only one without children, which I think is all to the good. Divorce is a terrible thing when there are kids involved.' Anna picked up her handbag and prepared for departure. 'Give my apologies to Simon—and watch out you don't fall a victim to his male charisma! He's got quite a reputation at the hospital for collecting hearts, so don't say you weren't warned.'

'I'm sure I shall be perfectly safe,' Wendy assured her, and was annoyed with herself because she had sounded stilted. 'But thanks for telling me,' she added. 'I know Debra's smitten with him, but I wasn't aware his path was littered with swooning nurses.'

Anna's dark eyes were dancing. 'I'm afraid I couldn't resist exaggerating a bit, but Simon has definitely had one or two girlfriends since coming to Stourwell. I have a friend at the hospital who tells me the current one is called Helen Barber and she's a staff nurse in A and E.' At the door she paused to wave her hand. 'Cheerio!'

The front door clicked shut and a moment later her car started up. Wendy listened until the sound had died away and then discovered her ears were still attuned to traffic noises. It was no good expecting to hear Simon's car for at least another hour, and she couldn't imagine why she had begun to think about it.

Opening her clothes cupboard, she debated what to wear. The evening was cool and her new cherry-red leisure suit seemed a good idea—casual and comfortable, and warm without being wintry. She untied her ponytail and brushed her hair energetically until it shone. After which she felt reasonably satisfied with her appearance and, at the same time, annoyed with herself because she had taken so much trouble.

It was nearly nine o'clock before a car drove in through the gateway and turned towards the cottage. Wendy allowed fifteen minutes instead of the ten Simon had stipulated, then went downstairs.

'You took your time,' he said as he opened the door. 'Where's Anna?'

It wasn't much of a welcome, but she could see the weariness in his eyes and there was a most unusual slight droop to his shoulders. He looked as though he had had a hell of an evening.

She explained about the other sister and went on, 'If you don't want to bother with a visitor——'

'What makes you think I don't want to bother?' He seized her by the arm and drew her inside. 'Don't you dare go flitting off because I didn't make you a pretty speech of welcome. Sit down and I'll get us both a drink. I'm not on call, so I can have anything I like. Whisky do you?'

'No, thanks.' Wendy repressed a shudder. 'Have you any sherry?'

'Of course I have.' He poured drinks for them both and handed her a glass. 'Cheers!'

They sipped in silence for a moment, then Simon put his drink down and gave a long sigh.

'There's something wrong, isn't there?' Wendy asked gently.

'You could put it like that.' He snatched at his

glass again and swallowed some more of the spirit. 'Nothing that a doctor shouldn't be able to take in his stride, but sometimes it hits you harder than others. We had two deaths.'

She waited, and after a while he started speaking again.

'One was an old bloke, a bad-tempered old so-and-so who bullied his poor little wife. No loss to anybody, you might think, but she was extraordinarily upset and cried all over me.'

Once more he stopped, and this time Wendy had to prod him to continue.

'And the other?'

'The other was a baby. She was born prematurely about three months ago and we had to fight hard for her life, but she did well and the parents were able to take her home eventually. Then she somehow picked up a chest infection and had to be re-admitted. Again we had to fight a battle to save her, and this time we didn't manage it. She died this evening.' He leaned forward and frowned down at his feet. 'Doctors never really get used to that sort of thing.'

'Nurses too.'

Wendy could recall incidents when she'd had to fight back tears and somehow find words of comfort for stricken relatives. Perhaps it was sometimes even worse for a doctor, because he bore a heavier load of responsibility.

She debated whether to dredge up the old hackneyed reminders about balancing one thing

with another—so few failures and so many suc-
cesses—but wisely decided not to insult his intel-
ligence with platitudes.

'The effects of other people's tragedies do wear
off,' she pointed out cautiously. 'Sometimes quite
quickly. We couldn't go on if they didn't.'

'How right you are!'

Had he spoken sarcastically? Wendy couldn't be
sure, and took refuge in drinking some more of
her sherry.

Simon had finished his whisky. 'Ready for top-
ping up?' he asked, getting up and waving the
bottle at her.

When she said she wasn't, he poured himself
another measure and began to sip it with considerably less urgency than he had displayed pre-
viously. He must be beginning to relax somewhat,
Wendy concluded, and wondered rather desperately what they could talk about now that the huge
subject of death seemed to have been disposed of.

She had quite forgotten the ostensible purpose
of her visit—to tell him more about her interview
with Mary Grieve—and said the first thing which
came into her head.

'I discovered this evening that Anna had been
married.'

'So?' Simon raised one eyebrow.

'I was surprised I didn't know, that's all. I'd
always heard her called Sister Templeton, or just
Anna. Somehow I never thought of her as having
a husband.'

'It's not a particularly rare state,' Simon pointed out. 'Anyway, she hasn't got a husband, only an ex.'

It was an absurd conversation and Wendy was wishing she had not begun it. She was considerably startled when Simon carried it on.

She was even more startled by what he said.

'Have you written me off as a bachelor? If so, you'd be wrong.'

CHAPTER FIVE

WENDY knew she ought to make some sort of comment—mildly interested and yet casual—but she could think of nothing.

Eventually she managed a feeble, 'Oh! Er—are you divorced too?'

The effect of the question was alarming. Simon leapt to his feet, nearly knocking over the small table on which his glass was placed.

'No, I'm bloody well not!' He glared at her so fiercely that she unconsciously shrank back in her chair. 'My wife died—three years ago—and our baby son died with her. They were both killed in a train crash. So you see, Wendy, I'm not a bachelor, though you may think I behave like one. I'm a widower. It's a hideous word, don't you think?— ugly and harsh—even worse than widow, and that's bad enough.' He began to walk up and down the room with agitated steps as he relived the agony of that evening.

'They were on their way to stay with Susie's parents. It was Easter and I was to join them briefly at the weekend, but I was only a house officer then and could get no more than one day free. I wasn't even able to see them off at Victoria, but I expected a phone call to say they'd arrived safely. I waited and waited, then I got a frantic call from my father-in-law to tell me about the crash. Nobody knew any details then. I went through agony before we knew for sure if they were among the casualties, and then—then we were told they were both dead. My darling Susie and little Jonathan—just names on a list.'

He covered his face with his hands. 'Three years ago,' he said in a muffled voice, 'but at this time of the year the memory seems as clear as though it happened yesterday.'

Wendy found herself on her feet without knowing she had risen. Acting entirely instinctively, she put her arms round him and held him close. She felt him bury his face in her hair, and for a moment they stood like that, motionless, wrapped round with the warmth and solace of physical contact.

Simon moved suddenly. Flinging himself back into his armchair, he pulled Wendy down with him on to his lap. His arms held her so tightly she could hardly breathe, but she understood he needed someone to hold like that and made no attempt to ease the pressure.

After a while he began to speak.

'Thank you for listening so quietly and letting me sound off like that without interruption. It was just what I was desperate for.' He paused, then shot a question at her. 'Do you believe in telepathy?'

Startled, she said cautiously, 'I'd require notice of that question.'

'Never mind. It's only that I've been getting the feeling rather strongly that there's something in your life that caused you great distress. I'm wondering if it's anything to do with that accident you had. Was anyone else involved?'

Wendy had to swallow before she could find her voice. 'My—my fiancé. He was—killed.'

She heard Simon draw in his breath sharply, then he exclaimed, 'So that's why you sometimes seem kind of—withdrawn! Poor Wendy—you know what it's like to lose someone you love.'

'It can't be as awful as losing your wife—and there was the baby too.'

'Perhaps not, but it helps you to understand how another person feels.' He kissed her closed eyes and she knew he must have noticed they were wet.

But as his lips found hers she was overwhelmed with a terrible sense of regret. The tears had not been of grief in the true meaning of the word, but simply emotion. She had never grieved for Vernon in the way everyone had imagined—her mother and grandmother, the neighbours, all her friends at the hospital. They had all been so kind, and she had felt such a hypocrite.

They had met at a disco and he had started dating her the next day. Before she fully grasped what was happening, she found herself engaged to him, an expensive ring on her finger but—strangely for such an impetuous young man—no talk of marriage. Gradually Wendy became aware of a growing sense of dissatisfaction. Small incidents showed her that Vernon wasn't quite the charming person she had believed.

Sadly, she began to think the engagement had been a dreadful mistake. Most uncharacteristically she had allowed herself to be swept off her feet, and the sooner she regained her equilibrium the better.

Then the accident happened. Deeply shocked because of the loss of a young man's life, and bitterly conscious that she had already lost her fiancé when the crash occurred, Wendy had gone along with the image expected of her and done her best with it.

One thing was clear in her mind. Never, never again would she allow herself to be conned into believing she was in love when all she really felt was physical attraction.

It had been a relief to escape to Stourwell, but now the past seemed to have caught up with her and she was again being forced into playing a part which didn't fit.

And yet she wasn't *really* being forced. She had only to break free from Simon's encircling arms and tell him the truth. Simple!

But it wasn't simple. She couldn't think while he was kissing her. Her brain felt as though it had been stuck together with glue and she was conscious only of her physical sensations. Besides, he had taken it for granted she understood his own suffering, and he had been comforted by sharing it with her.

How could she possibly fling at him the information that she wasn't—in the truest sense—suffering at all?

She was saved by the ringing of the telephone.

'Who the hell's that?' grumbled Simon. 'If somebody's forgotten I'm not on call——' He snatched up the receiver and listened for a moment. 'Oh, hello, Helen. Is anything the matter?'

Behind his back, Wendy's attention was caught by the sound of a car. Anna was returning. Smoothing her hair with her hands and hoping her make-up wasn't smudged, she moved to the door, managing to catch Simon's eye on the way. Pointing to her watch, she conveyed to him that it was time to leave, and if he thought her departure unnecessarily abrupt that was just too bad.

His eyebrows told her he was trying to signal something, but she ignored the message and slipped out of the flat, just quickly enough to reach her own flat before Anna opened the front door.

In the morning she was surprised to find a note had been pushed under her door.

Sorry about last evening, Wendy. I don't often make such a fool of myself. You must blame the whisky and try and forget about it as soon as possible.

It was good advice, but unfortunately she found it extraordinarily difficult to follow.

For a while life at Hillside followed a normal pattern. Mary Grieve, subdued but much calmer, left to stay with an aunt until she was fit enough for work. Other patients came and went without causing any disturbance.

Until one afternoon when Debra came racing to find Wendy in a state of great agitation.

'Sister! Oh, Sister, please come quickly! I've just found a patient lying on the bedroom floor. I—I think she's fainted, or perhaps she's dead. Oh, do please hurry!'

Wendy thought it unlikely that the situation was as serious as Debra imagined, but nevertheless she followed her at speed. Nurse Johnson was already there, kneeling beside the prone figure of an elderly woman who had only arrived yesterday and was convalescing after a hip replacement.

It was at once apparent that Mrs Scarfe, far from being dead, was not even completely unconscious, though she looked as though she might go into a coma at any minute.

'Thank goodness you're here, Sister!' Stella Johnson exclaimed. 'I don't think this is ordinary faintness.'

'Nor do I.' Wendy had remembered something. This patient was diabetic. 'It's probably either hyperglycaemia or hypoglycaemia,' she went on thoughtfully. 'The thing is—which?'

She heard Debra give a gasp of amazement at the long words, sounding so much alike, but reserved her explanation for later on.

'Mrs Scarfe!' she said urgently, taking one of the limp hands in her own and holding it firmly, willing the patient to respond. 'Did you eat your lunch?'

'I had a little soup——' The words were almost inaudible. 'Wasn't hungry.'

'She didn't have a proper breakfast either,' the nurse put in. 'Not much more than a cup of tea.'

'Sugar in it?' Wendy asked quickly.

'Never take it,' the patient mumbled.

'So you haven't really had anything since yesterday?'

Wendy was still using the same quiet, thoughtful tone, but behind her calm exterior her mind was racing. She turned to the pre-nursing student.

'Debra, go to the surgery and bring me my handbag. Be as quick as you can!'

Looking astonished, Debra fled, and a moment later returned with the large shoulder bag. Wendy searched it rapidly. Yes—she had been right, there was a small box of soft-centred chocolates, still half full, down at the bottom.

One at a time she fed them to her patient, and before long she had the satisfaction of seeing colour return to the wan cheeks as the faintness receded.

'It's like magic!' Debra breathed.

'Yes, but it's based on sound sense. Mrs Scarfe

had collapsed from lack of sugar, and that made her feel faint. In other words, she was suffering from hypoglycaemia, and as soon as I gave her some sugar she started to recover.'

Debra looked puzzled. 'But I thought diabetics weren't supposed to have sweet things.'

'They must have *some* sugar, but it has to be very carefully regulated. In this case the need was too urgent for worrying about how much to give.'

'You'll have to be more careful in future, dear,' Nurse Johnson admonished the patient as she helped her to her feet. 'And if you don't feel hungry and want to miss a meal, you must tell one of us, and we'll see you don't have an experience like this again.'

'I certainly wouldn't want to,' Mrs Scarfe agreed.

The small drama was over, but it had been a very real one, and Wendy spent twenty minutes giving Debra and Jane, the other student, a lesson on diabetes.

After that she had to go through it again for the benefit of Miss Greenfield, who had been absent attending a meeting at the hospital.

'I think we'd better get Simon to have a look at her,' the sister-in-charge said. 'It's not the threatened coma I'm worried about—that seems to have been dealt with very competently by you—but whether she did any damage to her hip when she fell. I'll see if I can get him bleeped. In the meantime Mrs Scarfe must be kept in bed.'

Simon did not arrive until Wendy was almost

due to go off duty, and it was Miss Greenfield who escorted him.

Wendy had seen little of him since that emotional evening when he had revealed to her the tragedy which had darkened his life. It was partly because she had deliberately avoided him—for some reason not entirely clear in her own mind—but mostly pure chance that they had not met except briefly and casually.

But this evening chance apparently decided on a change.

It had been a tiring day, with longer hours of duty than usual because it was Anna's free day. It was also unnaturally warm for May, with a hint of thunder in the air, and Wendy was glad when eight o'clock came. She walked dreamily and very slowly down the drive, pleased that it was down-hill and conscious of an aching ankle.

She had paused to admire a clematis with abundant small pink flowers which had climbed high into a small tree when she heard Simon's car start up, and immediately quickened her steps.

In spite of her attempt to hurry without appearing to do so—well nigh impossible—he caught up with her just as she left the main drive and leaned across to wind down the passenger's window.

'You were limping,' he accused.

Wendy was tempted to answer, 'So what?' but instead asked for his opinion of Mrs Scarfe.

'I'm not an orthopaedist, but the hip seems OK to me. I imagine she slid to the floor fairly gradually.' He engaged the gear lever. 'There doesn't seem much point in offering you a lift, so I'll go and park the car.'

The cottage was less than a hundred yards away, and they met again on the doorstep.

'How long have you been at Hillside?' demanded Simon, staring down at her feet.

'About three weeks,' Wendy said in surprise. 'What about it?'

'It's time your ankle stopped bothering you, that's what.'

'It's only because I'm tired.'

'You were saying that when you first came, and, though it may have been true then, it's now become a load of rubbish.' He unlocked the door and ushered her before him into the house.

She would have gone straight upstairs, but instead of that she somehow found herself in Simon's sitting-room.

'I wish you'd leave my ankle alone,' she said crossly.

'I've no intention of doing that. In fact, I'm going to prescribe a course of treatment.'

Wendy stared at him indignantly. 'You're not my doctor!'

'Are you registered with someone in Stourwell?'

'N-no, but——'

'Then I'm the nearest thing you've got to a doctor. The nurses at the hospital are looked after by an elderly and highly respected member of the medical staff, but I'm the only one who knows anything about Hillside, and *I* say something must be done about that ankle.'

'Like what? Physiotherapy?' she asked in a resigned tone.

Simon shook his copper head. 'I don't think it would help. Osteopathy was what I had in mind, but I'm afraid you wouldn't get it on the NHS. Would you mind paying for the treatment?'

'I wouldn't mind if it cured me.' Wendy had abruptly abandoned her obstructive attitude. 'Is there someone in Stourwell you can recommend?'

'There are two or three osteopaths in the city, but the only one I know anything about is the most distant and you'd have difficulty in getting there. It's a pity you don't drive.'

'I do, actually, but my car was a write-off——' She broke off and bit her lip. She hadn't wanted to remind him of the accident.

'Perhaps Anna would lend you hers.'

'I wouldn't dream of asking her.' Wendy tilted her chin, her eyes daring him to continue ordering her life for her.

'That independence of yours will land you in trouble one of these days,' Simon said darkly, scowling at her.

She smiled sweetly and made no comment, and he began to fumble in his pocket, eventually producing a pen and an old envelope.

'I'll write down the name for you, but I'm afraid you'll have to look up the phone number.' His voice was suddenly urgent. 'Don't put it off any longer, Wendy, love. You don't want to face the summer with a groggy ankle.'

Agreeing that she didn't, she took the envelope. Refusing his offer of a drink, she promised to ring the osteopath up at once.

'Good girl.' He gave her a pat on the head as though she had been a child.

It was nice of him to be so concerned about her tiresome ankle, Wendy reflected as she climbed the stairs. It must be because he was such a perfect physical specimen himself and so he couldn't stand other people being flawed.

At the telephone she read for the first time the name scrawled on the envelope. Ken Barber. She had heard the surname somewhere before, she thought vaguely, but did not pursue the elusive memory. After all, Barber was quite a common name.

Ken Barber had his surgery in a quiet street on the far side of the city. Having booked her appointment to fit in with her next day off, Wendy had no difficulty in getting there. She simply caught a bus to Stourwell—the local transport having turned out more reliable than Miss Greenfield had suggested—and spent an enjoyable morning wandering round.

When she had visited the cathedral and thoroughly explored the shops, she sought for and found the Regency Theatre Simon had told her about. Its Georgian façade was squeezed between an insurance office and an estate agents', and it would have been easy to walk past without noticing it. Peeping into the foyer, Wendy longed to see the auditorium, but the doors leading to it were closed.

So much exercise had made her hungry, and also caused her ankle to protest, so she combined a rest with eating a light lunch in a coffee-shop and then consulted a public map to find the best way of getting to her destination. It was not on a bus route, but the distance was not great and so she decided to walk.

Ten minutes later she was staring at a new-looking brass plate which informed her that Kenneth Barber DO MRO could be consulted there. Her ring at the bell was answered by a very pretty girl with a great deal of blonde hair falling over the shoulders of her white coat.

'Miss McBride? Please come in.'

Wendy was shown into a small but comfortable waiting-room with the receptionist's desk at one end. There was a pile of magazines on a low table, and she had no difficulty in finding one which interested her. As she turned the pages she gradually became aware that she was under close but surreptitious scrutiny from the girl at the desk.

Eventually the receptionist said in an elaborately casual tone, 'I see from your address that you live at Hillside Cottage.'

'Yes.' Wendy looked up, quite ready to talk. 'I'm a sister at the convalescent home.'

The girl's eyes dropped and she fiddled with the papers on her desk. 'I expect you know Dr Meadows.'

'Oh, yes, he's a neighbour.' Something in her interrogator's manner caused Wendy to add, 'But I don't see him all that often. He's very busy at the City Hospital.'

'I know. I work at the hospital too—a staff nurse.' Seeing Wendy's surprise, the girl hurried on, 'I'm just helping out here because my brother's receptionist was taken suddenly ill. I've got a week's leave, you see, so it was quite convenient.'

'It's very nice of you to spend your holdiay helping your brother.'

'I don't mind. I didn't really want to go away, but it's boring just staying at home when all your friends are working. This way I can see them in the evenings.' She paused, but Wendy made no comment, and after a moment she continued in a rather childish, confiding sort of way, 'I don't mean ordinary friends. Well, actually it's one particular friend I'm talking about. Simon Meadows.'

At that moment a fair-haired young man put his head round the door behind her, smiled at Wendy and said cheerfully, 'I'm ready, Helen.'

'If you'll just come this way.' His sister was on her feet and opening a different door leading into a corridor. 'The dressing-room is just along there. You'll find a robe hanging on the door.'

'I don't need to undress,' Wendy pointed out. 'It's my ankle I've come about.'

'Oh, I see. Well, just take your tights off, then.'

As she unpeeled her nylons, Wendy's mind was busy with the interesting information she had just received. Now, at last, she understood why the name Barber had seemed familiar. Anna had told her that Staff Nurse Helen Barber was Simon's current girlfriend.

She certainly had the sort of looks likely to appeal to a virile young man—almost perfect features and hair like pale spun gold—but even in one short conversation it had become clear that Helen hadn't very much else to offer—that she was, in fact, quite incredibly naïve.

The brother was good-looking too, with a much more attractive manner. He listened carefully to the history of Wendy's injury and wrote it all down. Then he assured her he thought three or four treatments would put it right.

'If you'll climb up on the couch,' he said, 'we'll get straight on with it.'

As she stretched herself out and looked at him expectantly, he added with a smile, 'You haven't asked me whether it's going to hurt. Most people do.'

Wendy laughed and admitted that the thought had crossed her mind, but she had been ashamed to put such an infantile question.

'I always try to avoid hurting my patients,' Ken assured her, 'and if it's necessary to do something a bit drastic—like a sudden jerk—I warn them beforehand. It's only momentary anyway.'

The treatment consisted of manipulation and massage. By the time it was over, Wendy felt as though her whole leg had been loosened up. The ache had vanished and been replaced by a wonderful sense of relaxation.

'How are you getting back to Hillside?' Ken asked as she slid cautiously off the couch.

'The same way as I got here—walk to the city centre and then get a bus.'

'If you wouldn't mind,' he said diffidently, 'it would be much better to have a taxi all the way. I don't want so much strain put on that ankle immediately after treatment. Helen will order one for you if you ask her.'

Meekly doing as she was told, Wendy reflected ruefully that her visit to the osteopath was turning out horribly expensive. On top of the fifteen pounds she had to pay Ken, there would be at least four pounds for the taxi, plus tip.

But if her ankle was cured, surely it would be worth it?

Putting the financial side out of her head, and still experiencing that wonderful feeling of relaxation, Wendy quite enjoyed the ride. She was paying the taximan outside the cottage when Anna came walking down the drive. She looked surprised to see Wendy getting out of a taxi, and was given a brief explanation.

'It's your turn now,' said Wendy. 'What are you doing here in the middle of the afternoon?'

'A patient spilt a cup of tea over me, so I had to

come back to change into a dry dress.' Anna displayed a soaking wet skirt. 'It was Mr Ferguson, and his Parkinson's is very bad today, so I couldn't blame the poor old chap.'

As they went into the house together, Anna continued speaking. 'I'm glad I've seen you. There's a meeting of the fête committee tomorrow and Miss Greenfield told me to ask if you'd take Marie's place on it. Apparently she keeps forgetting to mention it.'

'What fête committee?' queried Wendy.

'There's always a fête here in July, organised by the friends of Stourwell Hospital. It's quite a big event and raises a lot of money. Are you interested?'

'I don't know. I've never been on a committee and I know nothing about running a fête. Can't you take Marie's place instead of me?'

'I've done my stint. Besides, it will be nice for the other committee members to have a fresh face among them——'

'Who else is on it?'

'The chairman of the friends, naturally, and Miss Greenfield, and various people connected with the hospital. Simon is the only doctor.'

'Simon?' Wendy exclaimed. 'How on earth does he find the time?'

'He seems to manage. It's important for Hillside to be well represented or else the hospital contingent trample all over us. We have to stand up for our rights.'

'Such as?'

'You'll see,' Anna said vaguely. 'Can I tell Lavinia you're willing?'

'*Willing*?' echoed Wendy. 'Certainly not! But you can tell her you've coerced me into agreeing. It'll be a new experience, anyway.' Wendy paused outside her own door. 'Do we have to be busy on the day as well?'

'Gosh, you are ignorant! *Of course* we do, and we're all flat out by the end of it. The patients love it, though.'

As Anna disappeared into her flat, Wendy did a quick calculation. She was to see Ken again in two weeks' time, so, even if she had four treatments, her ankle ought to be all right well before the Fête.

It sounded as though she was going to need all her health and strength!

CHAPTER SIX

SIMON strode along the corridor linking the old and new blocks at Stourwell hospital with his hands in his pockets and his white coat flying open. The sun from the windows glinted on his head, emphasising the reddish gleam, but his tawny eyes had an inward look and his mind was not on the outside world.

He was worried about a patient who had developed hypostatic pneumonia since coming into hospital, something which he considered should not have been allowed to happen. The ward sister had been indignant, and they had parted frostily.

He was so deep in thought that the sudden bleeping coming from his pocket startled him, used as he was to it. There was a telephone quite close, and he made his way to it at once, glad to be distracted from the unsatisfactory situation he had left behind him.

But when he discovered who was on the line, his annoyance was merely switched into a different direction.

'Helen! You know I don't like being bleeped for personal calls. What do you want?'

'That's not a very nice way to speak to me,' she complained.

'I'm sorry. Is it anything important?'

'Yes, it is! I'm fed up. I'm on holiday this week and you haven't rung me once. I don't mind working all day, but I do expect to have a bit of fun in the evenings.'

'What on earth are you talking about?' Simon demanded. 'First you say you're on holiday and then you talk about working all day——'

'I'm helping out at my brother's surgery. His receptionist is ill. Incidentally——' her voice altered subtly '——one of the sisters at Hillside came to see Ken yesterday. A quiet sort of girl with a ponytail—not a bit like a sister.'

'Wendy McBride.'

'I think that was the name,' Helen said with elaborate casualness.

'Actually, I recommended your brother,' Simon told her. 'That ankle has been bothering her ever since she came, and I thought it was time it was put right.'

'It sounds as though you know her quite well.' Helen did not attempt to hide her jealousy.

'My dear girl, she lives in the same house! But I don't see all that much of her,' he added hastily, and went on to change the subject. 'Did you ring me up in the middle of the afternoon to have a good moan, or was there something else on your mind——'

'I thought we might go this evening to see the Country and Western programme on at the theatre—it only lasts for one week—and I'd love to see it.'

Simon's reply was swift and very positive.

'Sorry, love, but this evening is impossible. There's a fête committee, and you know I'm on that.'

'You don't *have* to be there, do you?'

'No, but I intend to, all the same.' He made an unsuccessful attempt to hide his impatience. 'If I don't go, I shall probably get landed with some ghastly job on the day, like organising the children's sports.'

'I don't see why,' Helen said sulkily.

'Well, *I* do, but I'll take you to the theatre tomorrow if you like. I'm not on call.'

They argued for a little longer, then Helen gave way, as he had known she would. Replacing the receiver, Simon wondered why the hell he had been so weak. What on earth was the point of trying to disentangle himself from Helen when he wasn't prepared to be brutal? Obviously if he wanted his freedom he would have to win it the hard way.

The trouble was he hated to hurt anyone, human or animal.

At the committee meeting Wendy felt very much a new girl. The chairman of the friends, a business-like man recently retired, made her a formal speech of welcome, then got briskly on with the agenda. They started without Simon, who came in fifteen minutes late and slid into his seat with a muttered apology. He said very little, though he did put forward a suggestion that the local ballet school should be asked to provide some of the entertainment, and this was agreed to.

Miss Greenfield firmly squashed a proposal that Hillside should undertake to organise the teas.

'You'd have the full use of our kitchens,' she pointed out, 'but it would be quite impossible for us to do such a big job. We just haven't got enough people available.'

Towards the end Wendy found herself offering to help with the raffle, which didn't sound too onerous for someone so totally inexperienced. Simon, she noted, skilfully avoided entangling himself with any of the activities, in case he wasn't free on the day.

They emerged from the house in a body and separated to their various cars. As Wendy prepared to set off down the drive on her own, she felt a light touch on her arm.

'It's a super night.' Simon gazed up at the star-studded sky. 'Much too good to waste by going straight indoors after being shut up in Lavinia's sitting-room for two solid hours. I'm going to leave my car here and go for a walk. Coming?'

'It does sound a nice idea,' she agreed. 'If you're sure you wouldn't rather go jogging.'

'I'm not dressed for jogging. How about a stroll round the lake?'

'Great! The ducks will be going to bed, and I love to hear them talking to each other.'

Wendy knew she was babbling from sheer tension, though why she should feel like that she couldn't imagine. As they began to walk slowly away from the house, into a different world of small rustlings and cheepings, gradually her spirit grew calmer. By the time they reached the lake, where the water shimmered gently in the faint light, she was feeling relaxed and at ease.

But then Simon slipped his arm into hers, setting her pulses racing, and she felt an urgent need to break the silence even if what she said was nonsense.

'I never can remember the difference between a moorhen and a coot. Can you?'

'Do you particularly need to know?' Simon enquired politely but with a ripple of amusement in his voice.

'Of course not, but I'd like to be able to distinguish them. They're so common around water it seems stupid not to know one from the other.'

'They're both black——' he began solemnly.

'I know that! But they aren't exactly the same.'

'One of them has a white patch on its head—I think it's the coot. Is that sufficient difference for you?'

'It would be if I could be sure it was correct, but you seem uncertain.'

Suddenly they were both helpless with laughter, and when they had recovered Wendy found her-

self sitting on a seat—had she collapsed on to it or
been steered there?—with Simon's arm round her
shoulders. It was so very enjoyable to feel it there
that she made no attempt to move.

For a few minutes they sat in silence, absorbing
the dusky beauty around them. Ducks were quack-
ing softly and in the trees small birds were settling
for the night with sleepy murmurings. A gentle
breeze stirred the rushes and fanned Wendy's
face, still flushed after the stuffy room.

'All it needs now is a nightingale,' Simon said
dreamily.

'That might be almost too much—I mean, everything's so lovely. Personally I'm quite content.'

'How rarely one can say that! Do you remember
the last time you were content?'

Wendy thought for a moment. She had been
pleased and excited when she landed the job at
Hillside, but that wasn't the same as being content.
And although she had enjoyed working there, the
tiresomeness of having an unreliable ankle had
caused a vague feeling of dissatisfaction.

'No, I can't,' she said eventually. 'Can you?'

'I'm not even going to try. It's a waste of time at
a moment like this.'

His arm round her shoulders tightened and she
could feel his hand gently fondling the bare skin
of her neck. The touch of his fingers sent shivers
of delight down her spine as the whole of her body
responded to his nearness and masculinity. When
the hand explored further, sliding down below the

neckline of the summer dress she had found time to change into, she eagerly anticipated a greater intimacy.

'Damn bra,' she heard him mutter, and the next moment the hooks were undone and his groping, sensuous fingers achieved their objective.

His free hand took hold of her chin and turned her face towards him. As his lips found and took possession of hers, Wendy felt herself floating on a cloud of physical sensation which aroused a crazy longing for total submission.

She had no idea how long they sat there. Twenty minutes? An hour? Time had ceased to exist and there was only the joy of giving and receiving the small, tender and yet passionate caresses of. . .

Of what? Certainly not love. She wasn't such a fool as to imagine that. What she was enjoying now could only be physical attraction, an ephemeral thing, wonderful while it lasted but leaving nothing behind it except a happy memory.

And so Wendy closed her eyes and allowed herself to drift, forgetting both past and future, and dwelling entirely in the present.

Suddenly they were both startled by an unearthly shriek from the lake. There was a tremendous splash and a half-seen bird skidded across the surface of the water, to vanish in a clump of reeds. Ripples spread outwards, twinkling in the starlight, and a lesser splash suggested that some small animal—a rat?— had dived into the water.

'What was that?' Simon released her reluctantly.

'A moorhen?' she suggested.

'More like a coot. I think I saw the white patch.'

They were both laughing as they disengaged themselves and returned to the real world, but it was only a fragile mirth. Wendy understood quite clearly that nothing had really changed in spite of the magic hand which night had laid on the park and its lake. Simon was still mourning the death of his wife and this passionate interlude had merely been an attempt to find consolation.

She had an uneasy feeling that the sooner she got that fixed in her mind, the better.

Hand in hand, they walked slowly towards the house, two people linked by physical contact but with their minds far apart. It was not until they reached his car that Simon seemed to remember she was still there.

'How did your ankle react to the first treatment?' he asked suddenly.

'Very well. The osteopath thinks he can get it right in about six weeks.' Wendy hesitated, then couldn't resist adding, 'There was a friend of yours acting as temporary receptionist. Apparently she's the osteopath's sister. Was that why you recommended Ken Barber?'

There was a small pause and then Simon said stiffly, 'I didn't recommend him. I said he was the only one I knew anything about, which was the truth. You found him OK, didn't you?'

'I don't know anything about osteopathy, so I

couldn't judge, but he was very nice and incredibly good-looking—just like his sister.'

Simon unlocked his car. 'Would you like a ride down the drive?'

'No, thanks.' Wendy glanced up at him and saw in the light streaming from the house that he was looking rather strained. 'How did you know I'd been to see Ken? Did Helen tell you?'

'I suppose she must have done—we sometimes run into each other at the hospital.' He bent his head and kissed her lightly on the mouth. 'Goodnight, Wendy. Sleep well.'

As she followed the red lights of his car down the drive, her mind was so full of the problem of Helen that she felt tiresomely wide awake.

How did she fit into the picture? Was she another 'consolation', or were Simon's feelings for her rather more serious?

On the day after the committee meeting there was an unusually large exodus of patients from Hillside, and for a brief while they had only thirty instead of the normal fifty.

Then the ambulance from Stourwell began bringing a new batch and the hall always seemed to be full of pale, bewildered people sitting surrounded by polythene bags and bulging holdalls. Debra and Jane, who were usually extremely helpful on these occasions, were both at college, so nurses and sisters toiled to sort out the confusion and restore confidence to the new arrivals.

'I'd got used to the hospital,' one of the women complained. 'Now I've got to start all over again.'

'Everybody likes Hillside, so I'm sure you'll soon feel at home here,' Wendy assured her.

The patient glanced out at the vista of trees and grass. 'It looks awfully like being in the country, and I never did care much for that. It isn't so easy for visiting either. My hubby doesn't drive, and that'll mean he's always got to get somebody to bring him.'

Fortunately the majority were delighted to find themselves at such an attractive place. Escorting an elderly man with a Zimmer up to the first floor in the lift, Wendy found he was a keen and knowledgeable gardener.

'I can't wait to get rid of this thing,' he confided. 'Looks as if you've got some interesting shrubs here, and as soon as I can manage with a stick I shall be off into the grounds.'

Wendy gave him a corner bed with a fine view of the park and returned to the hall to make sure no one had been overlooked. She found a slim dark-haired youth staring moodily out through the revolving doors.

'Where did you spring from?' she exclaimed.

'I've been outside. Didn't fancy being shut up with all that mob.' He turned slowly and gave her an uninterested look from a pair of very blue eyes in an ashen face.

'It was a bit crowded,' Wendy admitted tactfully. 'What's your name?'

'Sean Conway. Haven't you got any notes about me?'

'I expect they've gone to the office.' She glanced about her. 'Where's your luggage?'

'That's it.' Sean indicated a rucksack leaning against the side of a chair.

Wendy smiled. 'Are you setting off to walk the Pennine Way when you're better?'

'Good lord, no! That's not my scene at all. It's just an easy way of carrying my gear.' He changed the subject abruptly. 'What's it like here? Do you have wards?'

'We don't call them that. They're three and four-bedded rooms——'

'Shall I be in with all those old blokes?' Sean exclaimed in alarm. 'I couldn't stand it, Nurse—honestly!'

'You'll only have to sleep there.' She turned and led the way to the lift. 'I'm afraid we mostly get elderly males, because they're more likely to be the ones who don't have anybody to look after them at home.' Gently she added, 'Couldn't you have gone home to convalesce?'

'No, I couldn't! I got chucked out for insisting on trying to get work as an actor instead of going into the family business. The hell of it is I was on my way to a job when I got a sort of meningitis—not the dangerous kind——'

'Viral meningitis, probably.'

'If you say so. Anyway, here I am, and I've lost the bloody job and I'm fed up.' Sean heaved his pack viciously across the floor, nearly knocking over a chair.

Wendy would have liked to help him with it, but thought it better not to offer. As the lift rose slowly to the first floor an idea came into her head, and instead of taking Sean to one of the bedrooms she asked him to sit down on a chair outside the surgery.

'I'm just going to the office to get your notes. I won't be a minute.'

She sped down the back stairs and found Miss Greenfield sorting through the file of patients' notes which had come from Stourwell. Quickly she put forward her suggestion.

'Sean Conway's the only patient here under fifty. He's absolutely dreading being put in with all the old men. I wondered if he could have one of the single rooms? We've got two vacant.'

Miss Greenfield frowned. 'It sounds very much like preferential treatment.'

'But it would certainly be in the best interests of the patient. Besides, I wouldn't mind betting the older men don't want him in their room any more than he wants to be with them.'

'You're probably right about that.' The sister-in-charge searched for and found Sean's notes. 'I see he's only eighteen, and the poor lad won't find a single soul here he can fraternise with. I think we might stretch a point in his case and let him have his own room, but do make it clear he'll have to turn out if it's needed for an emergency.'

Upstairs again, Wendy relayed the good news to Sean, and was rewarded by seeing him smile. He really was quite good-looking when he wasn't scowling, she reflected as she showed him to his room. She left him sitting by the window, apparently too exhausted to unpack his rucksack. If either of the two teenage girls had been here he would have had help, but she herself was far too busy.

It would be a nice change for Debra and Jane to have a patient in their own age-group to help care for.

Working hard among the new patients, learning their names, the nature of their ailments or injuries, and the details of their medicaments, Wendy forgot all about Sean until lunchtime. He drifted into the dining-room, ate an unsociable meal and then vanished into the grounds. She saw him briefly at teatime, when she asked if he was comfortable in his room.

'Yes, thanks, Nurse.' Awkwardly he added, 'It was decent of you to fix it for me.'

'I was glad to do it.' She hesitated, then added casually, 'By the way, you call me Sister. The nurses are the ones in green uniforms.'

'Oh—sorry,' Sean muttered offhandedly. 'They're awfully old, aren't they?'

'You seem to have a fixation about people's ages!' Wendy laughed, and wondered how ancient she seemed to him. 'You'll be glad to know we have two pre-nursing students here quite a lot, but they're attending lectures at Stourwell College today. You'll see them tomorrow.'

The only answer was a shrug, and she was obliged to conclude that Sean didn't find the prospect of meeting the girls in the least cheering.

She was tired by the time she went off duty, but she found the cool evening air so refreshing that she was reluctant to go indoors. On an impulse she decided to do a little weeding in the tiny front garden at the cottage. Officially it was under the care of the Stourwell parks superintendent, but it was so small it tended to get overlooked. Both Wendy and Anna cared for it when they felt in the mood, but Simon took no interest at all.

Half an hour later, as she straightened her aching back, he drove up and called out to her caustically, 'You'll be going to Ken Barber about your bad back if you continue weeding in that position! Why on earth aren't you kneeling?'

'Since when did you become an orthopaedist?' she retorted. 'Anyway, my knees don't like the hard ground.'

'Then get yourself a proper kneeling pad.'

'I would if I did a lot of gardening, but it's only now and then.'

Simon let her have the last word and suggested a break for coffee. To refuse would be ridiculous, but Wendy was reluctant as she followed him into the house and went upstairs to wash her hands. The memory of that passionate interlude by the lake was still strong in her mind and heart, but she felt quite sure he had already forgotten it.

'I heard you'd had an influx of new patients,' he said as he handed her a mug.

'About fifteen, I think, but they seemed more! I don't think they've brought any problems with them. Except one, perhaps.' She gave him a brief account of her conversation with Sean. 'He's making it very plain he intends to resist any attempts by the other patients to get to know him. The men couldn't care less, but one or two of the women would like to mother him. He hasn't bothered much about politeness in fending them off.'

'Typical teenager.'

'They aren't *all* like that,' she argued.

'Have it your own way,' he said lazily. 'What's wrong with this particular one—medically, I mean?'

When she had told him about Sean's illness, she went on to mention some of the more interesting cases which had arrived at Hillside that morning.

'I suppose I ought to do a round and check up on them,' Simon said, 'but it doesn't sound urgent.'

They had exhausted the subject, and silence descended on them. As Wendy desperately searched for something else to talk about she heard the front door open.

'There's Anna!' she exclaimed.

Simon raised his eyebrows. 'So?'

'Oh—er—I thought you might want to ask her in for coffee.'

'How very kind of you!' The sarcasm in his voice stung her and she felt herself flushing. 'Were you afraid I wasn't capable of thinking of it for myself?'

'Of course not,' Wendy floundered hopelessly. 'I—I spoke without thinking at all.'

'Very unwise.' Simon unfolded his long limbs. 'But since you obviously find a tête-à-tête with me so difficult, I'll see if Anna would like to join us.'

Momentarily alone, Wendy wondered miserably what on earth was the matter with her. There was nothing about a romantic hour or so in the park which should have inhibited all ordinary human contact. Most people would enjoy it and then forget, so why couldn't she do the same?

It was a relief when Anna appeared and announced cheerfully that coffee was just what she was in need of. With her arrival the atmosphere in Simon's sitting-room changed completely and Wendy managed to recover her equilibrium. When the time came to leave he kissed them both impartially, his lips cool and strangely sexless, and shut the door on them.

'He's such a dear,' Anna said as they went upstairs. She glanced sideways at Wendy. 'I rather think he fancies you. Had you noticed?'

For a moment Wendy was too startled to think what to say, but somehow she forced a laugh. 'You wouldn't have thought that if you'd seen us before you turned up. We were all at sixes and sevens with each other. Both of us saying the wrong thing all the time.'

'I expect you were tired, and Simon too. Everybody's like that sometimes.'

The words were consoling and Wendy digested them in silence. 'Anyway,' she said eventually, 'he's got a girlfriend at the hospital, hasn't he?'

'Since when did that stop the average male from fancying someone else?'

It wasn't the reply she had hoped for. If only Anna had said she'd heard it was all over between Helen and Simon. . .

Wendy's mood changed again and the strange, smouldering anger which had troubled her intermittently all the evening burst into flame.

'I think it's despicable for a man to string along two girls at the same time. He doesn't have to be serious about either, but at least he shouldn't switch from one to the other like—like——'

'Like a bee going from flower to flower.' Anna burst out laughing. 'In my experience men are mostly like that. I'm afraid you've got a hopelessly romantic view of the opposite sex.'

'Of course I haven't! I just happen to believe in. . .' Wendy searched frantically for a word, but 'loyalty' was the only one which came into her mind, and it sounded so terribly pompous.

Simon, quite obviously, didn't believe in it.

Anna did not wait for her to finish the sentence. 'Anyway, we're very lucky to have Simon as a neighbour, in spite of his lack of principles.'

Wendy was not at all sure about the luck. If the occupant of the downstairs flat had been less attractive, she might have been spared her present mental turmoil.

Or, on the other hand, it might only be due to the discovery that Vernon wasn't all that she had imagined, followed by his tragic death. The combination of circumstances had made her vulnerable to any reasonably likeable man who happened to appear on her horizon. She had, in fact, been 'caught on the rebound'.

Whatever the cause, her growing feeling for Simon was definitely something not to be encouraged. In future, she resolved, she would do her best to avoid him.

It was her day off when he did a round at Hillside and they did not meet at all. For a while she even managed to dodge him at the cottage.

And then something happened which put her own worries out of her head.

CHAPTER SEVEN

WENDY had never got to know Jane, the quieter of the two teenagers, very well. Debra was an extrovert, ready to be friends with everyone, but Jane was much more reserved. Consequently Wendy was slightly surprised when the dark-haired prenursing student approached her as she came out of the office one evening after returning the keys of the drugs cupboard.

'Could I have a word with you, Sister, or are you too busy?' Jane asked diffidently.

'I can certainly spare the time to listen if you've got a problem,' Wendy said with a smile. 'Shall we go outside? We're not likely to be interrupted there.'

'It isn't exactly *my* problem,' Jane explained as they sat down on a seat facing the rose garden. 'I mean, it's certainly something I'm worried about, but it's nothing to do with me personally. Or does that sound terribly muddled?' She pushed back a wispy fringe and fixed Wendy with troubled eyes.

'It does rather! Suppose you begin at the beginning.'

'I feel horribly mean talking about Debra behind her back, but I do think somebody ought to be told, and you're the easiest one to talk to.'

'Thank you,' Wendy was touched by the tribute. 'What exactly is it about Debra that's worrying you?'

'She's been getting very friendly with that boy—Sean, I mean.'

'Surely there's no harm in that? He hasn't got anyone except you two who approximates to his own age.'

'He doesn't take any interest in me, but he does seem to like Debra.' Jane paused, swallowing nervously.

This time Wendy refrained from prodding. She was recalling several occasions during the last day or two when she had seen Debra in animated conversation with Sean, and once at least she had had to remind her of some duty she was neglecting. At the time she had been tolerant, glad that the awkward boy seemed happier, but now she began to feel slightly apprehensive.

'It was last evening,' Jane went on. 'We always cycle home together, and I waited ages for her. Eventually I got fed up and went to look for her, and she wasn't anywhere downstairs, so I went up and—and I found her just coming out of Sean's room. I noticed at once that she was looking all sort of flushed and excited and—and she was doing up the buttons of her dress. I asked her why she'd kept me waiting all that time, and she told me it was none of my business and I'd better belt up.'

Wendy had been listening in increasing dismay.

When she had persuaded Miss Greenfield to let Sean have a single room she had never anticipated having anything like this happen. At the moment she couldn't think of the best way to handle it, so she concentrated on calming Jane's perturbation.

'I'm very grateful indeed to you for telling me this. It can't have been easy to tell tales about your friend——'

'I felt it would be dreadfully wrong to keep it to myself,' Jane said earnestly.

'Well, don't let it worry you now you've shifted it on to my shoulders. Just treat Debra exactly the same as usual and leave it all to me.' Wendy hesitated, then added, 'I shouldn't think they were actually making love, but any sort of romantic situation involving a patient can't be allowed here—not in a bedroom, anyway, it's far too dangerous.'

It was gratifying to see Jane's relieved expression, but not so pleasant to have the ball definitely in her court. She ought to tell Miss Greenfield—she was well aware of that—but she liked Debra and didn't want to get her into serious trouble. If possible, she would handle it herself.

Although she had assured Jane that actual love-making was unlikely, the more she thought about it the less certain she became. On the face of it, it seemed a terrible risk to take, but at that time of the evening—with most patients watching television—was the risk so great after all?

Exactly as Jane had done, Wendy longed to

consult someone else, but the only possible person seemed to be Anna who, she had an uneasy feeling, might dismiss the whole thing as unimportant.

'It happens all the time,' she could imagine the other sister saying, 'so why bother?'

In the morning she had a stroke of luck.

Since her visit to the osteopath she had used the swimming-pool much more. Until then she had been afraid of making her ankle worse, but Ken Barber had told her swimming would be good for it. Consequently, whenever she got up early enough, she had a quick swim before going on duty, and nearly always she had the pool to herself.

That morning, she reckoned, there was time to do six lengths, and she went up and down at a leisurely speed, enjoying the rhythmic movement of her limbs and the caress of the water.

Suddenly, as she did a graceful turn at the deep end, she sensed someone watching her. Simon stood on the edge, his magnificent body clad in the briefest of swimming trunks.

'You're a very good swimmer,' he said, smiling.

'It's my only sport.' Wendy rubbed the water from her eyes and focused them on his face, ignoring what the unexpected sight of his near-nudity was doing to her emotions. 'Why aren't you jogging?'

'Two reasons. I got up too late to do my usual circuit of the park, and it's one of those airless sort of mornings when a swim really appeals.' He dived neatly over her. 'Race you to the other end!'

With his greater power, he won easily—assisted also by Wendy's extraordinary inability to control her breathing—and they hung on the rail side by side, their wet bodies almost touching. Cautiously, trying to be discreet about it, she moved a little further away. And knew at once that he had noticed.

Frantically searching for something to talk about, she remembered Jane's revelation about Debra and Sean. Why not ask Simon for his opinion?

'I wanted a word with you,' she began, though she hadn't until that moment thought of consulting him.

'I'm listening.'

In a few brief sentences she outlined the story, then waited for a comment.

'Why are you telling me?' Simon asked. 'Surely it's a matter for Lavinia to handle, or you could give young Debra a warning and hope she'll be sensible.'

'Teenagers aren't exactly noted for sense,' Wendy pointed out. 'Sean's very attractive in a gaunt sort of way and I think he could easily undermine any advice of mine. If Debra imagines she's in love with him——'

'Which she probably does.' Simon paused for thought, staring abstractedly through the glass wall of the swimming-pool, where a grey squirrel could be seen nibbling something it had found. 'I suppose I could drop a hint instead of you. It's just possible it might be more effective.'

'To Sean, you mean?'

'Heaven forbid! I was referring to Debra. I'm conceited enough to believe she used to have a yen for me. She might accept a word of warning from a man nearly old enough to be her father and yet young enough to remember how it feels to be a teenager. What do you think?'

Wendy was enthusiastic. 'I think it's a super idea! There's one snag, though. What will you say when she asks—as she inevitably will—how you know what she's up to?'

'I shall simply say someone saw her and leave it at that, and if she suspects Jane gave her away— well, they'll have to handle that themselves. I don't suppose Sean will be staying here long, and when he leaves it will all die a natural death.'

Cutting short Wendy's thanks, he flung himself backwards, kicking off vigorously from the side, and set off down to the other end at a great speed. She watched for a moment and then, remembering time was flying, hastily climbed out and went to the dressing-room.

As she rubbed energetically, she felt as though she were rubbing away not only the worry of Debra's behaviour but also the weight which had lain on her spirit ever since she had sat with Simon by the lake and they had come very close to making love. She felt freshened up, almost happy, though she could see no reason for it.

Unless it was because she and Simon seemed to have returned to the old friendly footing.

When she emerged from the dressing-room, clad now in jeans and a T-shirt, she found him just climbing out of the pool.

'Hang on a minute!' He put a wet hand on her bare arm. 'There's something I wanted to ask you, but all this teenage stuff nearly made me forget. I've got a couple of seats for the play at the Regency Theatre on Saturday evening and I've been hoping you'd occupy one of them. I don't believe you've visited it yet, have you?'

Wendy shook her head, and her hair, which had been screwed up into its topknot during her swim, swung out round her face and hid her expression—which was just as well, she couldn't help thinking.

'I'd love to, Simon. What's the play?'

'A Noël Coward revival—I forget which one. That's a date, then?'

'It certainly is.'

Delighted at this further proof that they were friends again, Wendy had not hesitated. She listened to his instructions regarding the time she was to be ready, then hurried off to change into uniform.

'What a horribly heavy sort of morning,' Anna complained as they set off together a little later.

'It's going to be one of those sweaty sort of days when you keep longing to dive under the shower.'

'I feel fine at the moment,' Wendy said gaily, 'but I expect that's because I've been swimming.'

She was free from lunchtime on Saturday and the whole afternoon could be devoted to preparing for her date with Simon.

She washed her hair and dried it in the sun, had a long lazy bath in scented water, then spent some time in choosing what to wear. Eventually she selected a summer dress with a pretty pattern of leaves on a blue ground. It was sleeveless, with a V-neck back and front, and she decided to carry a white lacy shawl in case it was cold after the theatre. Long silver earrings with a matching necklace completed the picture.

She was all ready, and it was only six o'clock, with Simon not yet home.

Holding a book in her hand but not concentrating on it, Wendy listened for the sound of his car. It was a relief when she heard it—you could never be sure that a doctor would be able to keep an appointment—and she knew she had only to get through the next twenty minutes and they would be off.

There was time to ask herself just why it was she had got into such a state of excitement over a simple invitation to see a play with a male friend. It must be, she decided, because it was so long since she had been dated at all—not since Vernon's death.

And, of course, she was very much looking forward
to seeing the famous theatre.

Punctually at seven o'clock, Simon, wearing
fawn lightweight trousers and jacket, with a cream
silk shirt and his hospital tie, came upstairs and
tapped on her door. When she opened it he looked
her up and down and gave a low whistle.

'What's happened to Sister McBride?'

'I drowned her in the bath,' Wendy said solemnly, and they both burst out laughing.

It was a good beginning to the evening, and
they continued to be at peace with the world and
each other. Simon found a parking space without
hassle and they strolled to the theatre with
comfortable time to find their seats.

A steady stream of people was pouring in
through the wide-open doors, and Wendy found
herself in a small foyer with walls covered in
striped Regency paper in white and crimson. They
went up some steps leading straight into the small
semi-circular auditorium at balcony level. The
whole area was divided into wedge-shaped sec-
tions rather like boxes without the drapery and
containing several rows of seats. Theirs were in
the front row, directly facing the stage.

'I've never seen anywhere like this.' Wendy
looked round her appreciatively.

'I told you it was very nearly unique.' Simon
presented her with a programme and a box of
Belgian chocolates. 'I'll go and order our drinks for
the interval. What would you like?'

That important matter settled, he vanished for a few minutes, and Wendy continued to study her surroundings. It was, she noted, a surprisingly young audience, perhaps because it was Saturday night. A lot of them wouldn't have been born when Noël Coward was writing his plays, but when the performance began she soon found that his wit and gift for comedy were as easy to appreciate now as long ago.

Simon had ordered their drinks for the second interval, and when the time came they made their way slowly, his hand beneath her elbow, up to a higher floor where the bar was situated.

It was crowded, but they managed to squeeze themselves into a corner. All around them people greeted friends, discussed the play and generally added to the babble of voices. Wendy was content to sip her Campari in silence, but Simon was hailed by a man of about his own age, also, apparently, from the hospital. He half turned his back, making no attempt to introduce Wendy, though, owing to the crush, she thought nothing of it at the time.

They briefly discussed the play and she half-listened without much interest. Then, suddenly, the conversation became personal.

The stranger said, 'I suppose you're in the balcony as usual?'

'Oh, yes—I think they're the best seats from the point of view of seeing and hearing, and that's what we're here for, after all.'

'My wife prefers downstairs. Can't say I agree with her, but it's not worth arguing about.'

There was a slight pause and Wendy got the impression he was trying to see over Simon's shoulder, but, as he was shorter, he was unsuccessful.

'Helen with you?' she heard him ask.

'Not tonight. She's on duty.'

At that moment the bell sounded and there was a general movement towards the door. Hidden behind Simon's tall figure, Wendy moved with the crowd and did not catch even a glimpse of the other doctor.

Not that it mattered what he looked like. His voice had managed to shatter her fragile happiness into tiny fragments about her, and she didn't know how she was going to get through the rest of the evening without giving herself away.

Yet nothing had really changed. She had been crazy enough to live, for a short time, in a fool's paradise, that was all. She had known all about Helen, so why had she allowed herself to close her eyes to the fact that she was only a substitute tonight for Simon's regular girlfriend? He had probably booked the seats for the two of them and then discovered Helen was on duty, so he had looked around for someone to take her place.

Somehow, by an effort of will, she gave an appearance of being absorbed in the third act. She clapped as enthusiastically as everyone else at the end, then walked out of the theatre in a daze.

'I don't know about you,' Simon said, 'but I didn't have time to eat before we came out. How about a pub snack on the way home?'

It was the last thing Wendy wanted, but she could think of no reason for not agreeing, any more than she could find a way to avoid walking hand in hand with him as they made their way to the City Arms. Cramped and dark, it was situated in a narrow alley near the cathedral. Its medieval beams were undoubtedly genuine, but the candle-light was artificial and the noise almost equalled that in the bar at the theatre.

Whether her change of mood had somehow conveyed itself to Simon she had no means of knowing, but conversation seemed difficult, and it was to ease the flow that she asked him about Debra.

'Have you managed to speak to her about Sean?'

To her dismay he shook his head. 'I haven't had a chance. As a matter of fact, I can't think why I suggested it. You know how rarely I'm at Hillside, and Debra isn't there all the time either.'

'Oh, dear, I hoped it had all been dealt with. For all we know, she may have paid another visit to Sean's room and——'

'She isn't under age, is she?' he asked.

'N—no, I don't think so, but——'

'So really it's up to her.' He held up his hand as Wendy started to protest. 'Don't get me wrong. I agree with you she shouldn't be carrying on with a patient, but I'm not sure it's quite the serious crime you seem to think.'

Though she hadn't realised it, Wendy had been looking for an excuse to quarrel with him ever since the evening to which she had so much looked forward had turned sour on her. Now he had given her an opportunity, and she snatched at it.

'I do think you might have told me you didn't think it likely you'd be able to speak to Debra——'

'Couldn't you have worked that out for yourself?' Simon asked coolly.

'Why should I? You sounded quite confident when you made the offer, and I was glad to leave it to you. Now time has been wasted and nothing done. If I hadn't chanced to ask, I suppose you'd have let it drift on until perhaps something really serious happened.'

'No, I wouldn't. I hadn't forgotten about it, as you seem to imagine. I was just waiting for an opportunity.' He laid down his knife and fork and drank some lager.

'In the meantime Debra may get herself landed with an unwanted pregnancy,' Wendy said angrily.

'In these days? Surely you're being unnecessarily pessimistic?'

The disagreement which was to have relieved her feelings was bringing her nothing but unhappiness, but somehow she forced herself to continue.

'Unwanted pregnancies are always happening. Kids aren't nearly as sophisticated as you seem to think.' She tossed her hair back and flung him a challenging look across the table.

Simon did not reply for a moment and then he said, 'You're very argumentative tonight. Are you deliberately trying to give me indigestion?'

Wendy had smiled before she could stop herself. She hesitated, then said curtly, 'I'm sorry. Shall we talk about something else?'

'With pleasure.'

But though both made an effort, the conversation continued to limp from one subject to another. Wendy was glad when the time came to leave the City Arms and make their way to the place where they had left the car. This time they did not walk hand in hand, and, when she remembered how happy she had been before that fatal visit to the theatre bar, Wendy felt tears welling up in her eyes and it was as much as she could do not to let them fall.

Soon—very soon now—the horrible evening which had started out so well would be over. But she was wrong about that.

They were silent as they drove through the city. Wendy, lost in thought, did not at first notice that Simon had taken a different route from the normal one to Hillside. She was still not very familiar with the city, and they had emerged on to a completely unrecognisable main road before she became aware that their surroundings were not what she had been expecting.

As she hesitated whether to mention it, he swung the car down a much narrower side-road which brought them quickly into the country. And suddenly her heart started beating so rapidly she was afraid he would hear it.

Simon was driving very slowly now, and when they came to a large empty field he turned into it and switched off the engine. There was no sound except the murmur of traffic on the distant main road. Rigid and tense, Wendy waited for what was going to happen.

At first nothing did. Simon leaned back in his seat with an air of relaxation, and she wished she could feel the same.

Eventually he said, 'It would have been a pity to drive straight home, don't you agree?'

Wendy wanted to say, 'I'm not at all sure I do,' but the words stuck in her throat. Instead she ignored the question and asked him where they were.

'Stapleton Woods Nature Reserve, or, to be quite accurate, the car park attached to it. Shall we get out and have a stroll?'

'Through the reserve?' She was alarmed for more than one reason. 'It'll be too dark to see the path—if there is one.'

'Of course there is—several, in fact—but I agree it might be rather too dark for comfort.' Simon looked up into the sky where a youthful moon played hide-and-seek with a succession of small clouds. 'I'm afraid it's not big enough to give much light. Let's wander over to the gate and see what it's like.'

Wendy could think of no good reason for refusing, and she did not resist when he took her arm and led her across the short, rough grass to the dark mass of trees ahead. Before long a wide gate, with a stile beside it, blocked their way. Side by side, they leaned on it and peered into the mysterious world beyond. As their eyes adjusted they saw a narrow path winding away between banks of brambles.

'One false step,' said Simon, 'and you could easily get yourself so entangled it might be difficult to get away. I guess we'd better stay on this side.' He put his arm round her and drew her close.

Wendy thrilled to his touch, but she was still struggling to keep her resolution, and she started to say, 'Simon—please!' when her mouth was closed by the pressure of his.

She forgot how angry he had made her by inviting her to the theatre merely because Helen couldn't come. Her will power melted like mist in the sun, and she allowed herself to be swept along on a flood of emotion.

And then, quite suddenly, the silence was broken by the most glorious sound she had ever heard. They drew slightly apart, listening.

Having tried out a few practice trills, the nightingale burst into the full beauty of its song; superb outpourings of music rippled through the trees and turned the nature reserve into a place of wonder and magic.

'I've never heard a nightingale before.' Wendy sounded almost awe-stricken.

'I believe this place is famous for them, but I didn't dare to hope we'd be that lucky.'

They stood quietly, still with their arms round each other but with their attention fixed entirely on the unseen singer. The bird seemed tireless, pouring out its tiny heart in a paean of praise, singing just for the sheer joy of being alive.

The concert ended at last and the spell was broken. Exhausted by so many different emotions, Wendy felt she wanted only to be taken home, and Simon made no attempt to resume what the nightingale had interrupted.

It was as they turned away from the gate that they heard a new and quite different sound.

CHAPTER EIGHT

WENDY had been anxious to escape from the dangerously romantic vicinity of the wood, but now she stopped abruptly.

'What was that?'

'It sounded like a cat.' Simon cocked his head in a listening attitude.

'Out here in the woods? Surely it can't be! We're nowhere near a house, are we?'

'Not as far as I know.'

Both listened intently, and the sound came again. This time it seemed nearer, and there was no doubt about what it was.

'It must be lost, poor little thing.' Wendy leaned over the gate and began to make enticing noises likely to appeal to a cat. 'Whatever can have made it travel so far from home?'

'It could have been dumped,' Simon suggested. 'People do that sort of thing to unwanted animals, and they probably reasoned—if they thought at all—that it would find plenty to eat in a nature reserve——' He broke off as a small slinky shadow emerged from the blackberry bushes and stood hesitating in the middle of the path. 'There it is!'

Wendy began to climb cautiously over the stile, talking quietly to the cat as she did so. As she reached the leafy carpet, she gave a sudden exclamation. 'Simon! It's holding one of its front paws up—I believe it's hurt.'

'Perhaps there's a thorn in it. Er—what exactly are you planning to do?'

Wendy turned an astonished face towards him. 'Take it home with us, of course. What else could we do?'

'The RSPCA copes with lost animals.'

'I don't know if it's possible to contact them as late as this, and I'm sure you wouldn't want to drive round trying to find out. I can't see we've got any option but to take it with us.'

'Yes, we have. We could leave it here.'

'You can't be serious!' she protested.

'Perhaps not, but even if we take it back with us to Hillside for the night we're landing ourselves with all sorts of problems.'

'Not you,' Wendy retorted. 'Me. But I'm used to cats and I don't mind at all.'

Simon did not pursue the argument, and Wendy marvelled at her relief because his momentary callousness had not, apparently, reflected his true feelings.

Advancing slowly, she held out her hand, and was delighted to see the little creature limp towards her. A gentle stroke produced the hoped-for response of a raised tail. Hesitating no longer, she picked the cat up and cradled it in her arms, where it nestled with so much confidence that she knew it must have known a happy home.

Back on the other side of the stile, she displayed her capture to Simon, and he was immediately concerned about the injured paw.

'I believe it's broken.' He felt it gently. 'No wonder the cat's so thin! It must have been finding it difficult to hunt.'

'Can you set a cat's paw?' Wendy asked as they walked towards the car.

'The RSPCA will see to that.'

'But that will take time, and we don't know how long the paw's been broken. Besides, I'm on duty nearly all day tomorrow. The sooner the fracture's dealt with, the better.'

Simon grinned, and she knew his resistance had crumbled. 'When I was about twelve I thought I wanted to be a vet, but I never imagined a situation would arise years later when I had to practise veterinary surgery.'

'I expect an animal's paw is constructed much the same as a human leg.' Wendy climbed into the car with care and settled the cat on her lap. 'What shall we call it?'

'Does it have to have a name?'

'Of course it does. We can't call it "it" all the time.' Wendy thought for a moment. 'The trouble is we don't know its sex.'

'How about Stapleton—after the woods where we found it?'

'I think that's terrible! It's much too long for a little creature like this.' She lapsed into silence again, then exclaimed with a suddenness that startled him, 'Bramble! That's what I'm going to call it.'

'Now that you've named it,' Simon said, 'you're going to find it harder to part with it.'

Wendy thought so too.

The cottage was dark and silent, and Wendy remembered that Anna had announced her intention of spending the night at her home in the city.

'Come into my flat,' Simon said, 'and I'll see what I can do about this paw. You do realise it's going to be rather a hit-or-miss sort of repair without an anaesthetic? All I can do is straighten the bone, fix a splint and hope for the best.'

He began to collect the various things he would need while Bramble limped round the room, conscientiously exploring every inch. He—or she—when seen in a good light had turned out to be a pretty little animal with tabby stripes, a black nose and white shirt front.

'What will you use for a splint?' Wendy asked. 'A pencil?'

'I'd rather have something flat.'

In the end he found a ruler and, with some difficulty, cut off the required length. When everything was ready both he and Wendy scrubbed up—automatically in her case, since her role would require only that she held the animal as still as possible. At first this was a problem, until she managed to get a firm grip on the scruff which rendered Bramble almost helpless.

Until then she had been concentrating on this totally unexpected situation. Now, suddenly, all the emotions which had been driven away by the discovery of the lost cat came flooding back to overwhelm her. Simon was so close, his downbent head nearly touching hers. She could hear his breathing—so calm and steady—and was once again afraid he would notice the unevenness of her own.

She simply *must* avoid in future all those circumstances in which he could arouse in her nameless longings which were better left undisturbed. The resolution to keep away from him which had recently been made—and broken—had just got to be adhered to!

Hadn't she suffered enough—in a different way—over Vernon? So why invite another disaster?

'Looks as if you've made a good job of it,' she congratulated Simon when he had finished.

'Only time will prove, or disprove, that.' He began to tidy up. 'Have you got something you can use for a bed? If not, I think I can find a box about the right size.'

'I'd be grateful if you could.'

While he was rummaging in the kitchen Wendy soothed the cat, whose feelings had been greatly ruffled by its recent experience. As she felt the soft fur beneath her fingers and heard its first faint purr, she realised with sudden and complete clarity that she had never really had any intention of letting Bramble go to the RSPCA. She was going to keep it herself.

She told Simon as soon as he returned with the box, and found that she had totally failed to surprise him.

'I hope you're not acting on impulse, without going into it thoroughly in your mind,' he said dubiously. 'You won't be able to let the animal out for a day or two, which means a litter tray——'

'I told you I'm used to cats. I know exactly what I'm letting myself in for.'

'If you like, I'll go into Stourwell and find a shop which is open on Sunday,' Simon offered. 'I can stock you up with food and anything else you need.'

'That's really very nice of you.' Wendy was genuinely grateful. 'Specially as you don't approve.'

'I'm much kinder-hearted than I appear,' he told her blandly.

They went upstairs together and he unlocked the door while Wendy held the cat. As Bramble started on another tour of inspection, they stood looking at each other, both aware of the strange restraint which had fallen on them.

Suddenly Simon put his hands on her shoulders and looked deep into her eyes. Held by his gaze, she found herself quite unable to interpret it. Puzzled? Reproachful? Or could it possibly be tender?

She said quickly, 'Goodnight, Simon. Thank you for the theatre and—and everything.'

'Did we go to the theatre earlier this evening? I'd almost forgotten, it seems so long ago.' He kissed her lightly. 'I won't forget the shopping, that's for sure. See you tomorrow.'

Since she was on duty all day, it seemed unlikely, but it was not of the immediate future that Wendy was thinking as she got ready for bed. And as she sought in vain for sleep, it was the memory of the unknown doctor who had asked, so naturally and casually, 'Helen with you?' which disturbed her rest.

Sunday was a peaceful day. The cat spent most of it recovering from its ordeal in sleep, and at the convalescent home the patients were equally quiescent—taking part in a short morning service, watching television and—in some cases—strolling in the grounds. None of them required medical attention, and Simon remained invisible.

Wendy returned to the cottage after lunch to check on Bramble and noticed his car was missing, but outside her door she found a dozen tins of cat food, a bag of litter and a tray. There was also a small toy mouse, which brought a smile to her lips.

She must owe him quite a lot, she reflected, and was glad to find most items had a price on them. Before returning to duty, she put a ten-pound note into an envelope and pushed it under his door, with a brief note of thanks.

The following morning she found the same envelope outside her own door, containing a small quantity of change.

So far it had been quite extraordinarily easy to keep to her resolution not to have any personal contact with Simon, and she told herself emphatically she hoped things would stay that way.

But on Tuesday events at Hillside made that impossible. A patient fell downstairs.

It was Mr Mallory's own fault. An elderly man, and inclined to be cantankerous, he was recovering from a fall in his own home and also had heart trouble which made him liable to dizziness. He had been absolutely forbidden to use the stairs, but it was not considered necessary to escort him into and out of the lift.

Mr Mallory disliked being told what he could and could not do. Having got out of bed 'on the wrong side', as Nurse Johnson described it, he made up his mind he was now perfectly capable of walking downstairs.

Anna had a free morning and Wendy was taking surgery. She had just finished re-dressing a badly grazed elbow when the door burst open and Debra shot into the room.

'Sister! Can you come? Something terrible's happened!' And she added with all the dramatic effect of which she was capable, 'Mr Mallory's fallen downstairs!'

Wendy's busy fingers paused, but it was to the patient she spoke. 'I think that will be more comfortable, but have it checked at surgery tomorrow.'

The wide-eyed patient nodded and departed. As soon as she had shut the door with herself and Debra in the corridor, Wendy turned to the excited student.

'You really mustn't burst into the surgery like that unless there's a fire. I know you're not really a nurse, but it's not too soon to start exercising restraint.'

'Yes, Sister—sorry Sister,' Debra gabbled over her shoulder as she scurried ahead.

They came to the top of the stairs and looked down. Mr Mallory lay on his back, spreadeagled on the black and white tiles of the hall. Two nurses were on their knees beside him, and a semi-circle of patients registered varying degrees of shock.

Reaching the bottom of the stairs, Wendy turned to the student and gave rapid instructions. 'Please persuade everybody to go into the big lounge, then close the door and stay with them in case anyone feels faint. There's nothing they can do here, and some of them look very shaken indeed.'

Debra looked disappointed, but obeyed at once. Silently, the two nurses made way for Wendy to join them. With growing concern she looked for and failed to find a pulse, and her fingers on the carotid artery in the neck discovered no sign of life.

With a swift movement she directed a sharp blow at the region of the diaphragm, and Nurse Johnson, correctly interpreting a glance, started mouth-to-mouth resuscitation. They laboured for some time, working alternately in a steady rhythm, and timing their efforts carefully, pausing every now and then in the hope of detecting returning life.

Eventually they stopped and looked at each other, and Wendy gave a slight shake of the head.

'Has Miss Greenfield been told?' she asked.

'She wasn't in the office,' Stella said, 'and there was no time to go up to her flat.'

Miss Greenfield, who always breakfasted in her own domain on the second floor, invariably returned there later on for her mid-morning discussion with the sisters over coffee. It was, in a way, similar to the daily report in hospital.

'Someone must fetch her,' said Wendy.

'I'll go.' Nurse Baker, slim and still under fifty, started up the stairs at speed.

The other two waited silently until Stella said abruptly, 'We've hardly ever had a death at Hillside. I can't remember the last time. What do you think will happen now?'

'We can't assume Mr Mallory is dead until a doctor confirms it. I suppose we should have phoned for an ambulance immediately, but there didn't seem to be time to do anything except start trying to resuscitate him.' Wendy paused to review her recent conduct and felt the first stirrings of unease. 'I should think Miss Greenfield will send him to A and E now, where he'll be certified dead on arrival. That ought to be the end of it as far as we're concerned.' At least I hope so, she added silently.

At that moment the sister in charge came hurrying downstairs, followed by Nurse Baker.

'You've tried resuscitation?' she asked sharply.

'Yes, Miss Greenfield,' Wendy said, 'but without result.' On that point at least she felt secure.

'Why on earth wasn't I told about this immediately?'

'You weren't in the office——'

'But you all knew where I could be found.' Interrupting Wendy's attempted explanation, she swept on, 'There's no time to go into the matter now, but I must say it seems very unsatisfactory. The most important thing is to get Mr Mallory moved from this very public spot. The other patients must now be our primary concern.' Miss Greenfield turned to the younger nurse. 'Nurse Baker, please go and fetch Alf—and tell him it's urgent.'

Hillside employed a man to attend to the boiler and do all the odd jobs which the cleaning and kitchen staff considered beneath or beyond them. Alf was a genial giant of a man, willing to tackle anything.

'There's a stretcher in that store-room next to the office,' Miss Greenfield said as they waited. 'I think we can manage to move him on that, though

I'm afraid he'll have to be put in the store-room too. There simply isn't anywhere else. After all, people aren't supposed to die at convalescent homes.' She glanced at the hall clock. 'I hope Alf won't be long. We can't keep everybody shut up in the lounge much longer. I'm sure at least half of them already want to use the toilet.'

It seemed an age before the porter was located, but as soon as he arrived he briskly assessed the situation and announced that he could move Mr Mallory without help.

'A little old gent like that—I can pick him up in my arms.'

'I couldn't possibly permit any such thing,' Miss Greenfield said firmly. 'The body must be moved with dignity. If you take one end of the stretcher and the two nurses the other, I'm sure there'll be no difficulty.'

It was soon done, and she locked the door and put the key in her pocket.

'Are you going to send for an ambulance?' Wendy ventured to ask.

'Not at present. I intend to consult Dr Meadows if I can get hold of him. Certainly a doctor must certify that death has taken place, but I don't want the other patients to be distressed by seeing a covered stretcher—and someone is *sure* to see it— being carried out in daylight.'

No one made any comment and, ignoring the two nurses, Miss Greenfield continued addressing Wendy. 'I'd like you to come to the office, Sister, and give me a full and frank account of this disturbing matter. It seems there's a good deal which requires explanation.'

Outwardly calm but inwardly considerably worried, Wendy had to wait while a call was put through to Simon.

After stating the bare facts, Miss Greenfield went on, 'I should greatly appreciate it, Simon, if you could find time to come over.'

Wendy held her breath. Would he ask why the hospital was only now being contacted? Apparently he did not raise the matter, for the conversation ended almost immediately.

'He'll try and get here by lunchtime,' the sister-in-charge reported. She fixed Wendy with an accusing eye. 'And now, Sister, I'd like to hear what you have to say.'

Wendy made out as good a case for them all as she could. Debra—who had witnessed the fall—had kept her head and fetched a sister, after which she had been put in charge of the patients incarcerated in the lounge. One of the nurses had looked for Miss Greenfield and, failing to find her, had returned to where the body lay to see if she could do anything to help.

The sister-in-charge frowned. 'After you arrived, Sister, there was no need for *both* the nurses to remain. Why was one of them not sent up to my flat?'

Wendy decided to be frank. 'I think it was because we were concentrating on trying to revive

Mr Mallory. Nurse Johnson helped me with the resuscitation, and I suppose I kept Nurse Baker in case she required relieving, but I didn't work it out. Quite honestly, I didn't think of sending her to fetch you, but I now realise I should have done so.'

'I understand the situation,' Miss Greenfield said thoughtfully, 'but I still find it unsatisfactory. I'm quite sure Dr Meadows will not approve.'

It seemed more than likely to Wendy too, and her heart sank. Somehow it felt worse to have earned Simon's displeasure than to be reprimanded by the nursing officer—which made no sort of sense.

'Are you on duty this afternoon?' Miss Greenfield was asking.

'I have two hours free after lunch.'

'I should be obliged if you'd hold yourself available for questioning in case Simon's late. You never know with doctors.'

When Wendy emerged from the office she found the two nurses hovering, and they immediately pounced on her.

'What did she say to you? Was she very angry?'

'She certainly wasn't pleased, though she saw my point of view—I mean, about being anxious to get on with the resuscitation.' She put them both fully in the picture. 'Have you told anybody the truth about Mr Mallory?'

'One or two people asked, and there seemed no point in trying to hush it up. Luckily they seemed to assume he'd been whisked away by ambulance while they were shut up in the lounge.'

'I wish he had been,' Wendy sighed. 'I'm not at all looking forward to the official enquiries.'

Simon arrived when they were all at lunch. He seemed in a hurry and for once took no interest in the good food provided at Hillside. Beckoned by Miss Greenfield, Wendy left the dining-room and followed her to the office.

Simon was standing with his hands in his pockets, staring out of the window, but he swung round at their entry, his face very serious.

'It was good of you to come so quickly,' Miss Greenfield said formally.

He ignored the remark and plunged straight into practical matters. 'Before I view the body, what have you done about next of kin?'

'Nothing so far.' Her businesslike tone matched his. 'Mr Mallory is—was—a bachelor and his only relative is a nephew in America.'

'Then presumably his solicitor will take charge?'

'I imagine so. Would you like to see him now?'

'Yes, please.' His voice changed suddenly and became more natural. 'Where on earth have you put him? I know your lift is too small to take a trolley.'

'We don't possess one anyway. People who come to convalescent homes are supposed to be fairly mobile. But we did manage to find a stretcher and the porter helped us to put him in the store-room. It was the best we could do.'

'Good God!' Simon exclaimed. 'How very unsuitable, but I suppose you had no alternative.'

Wendy stayed behind while they were next door. Her thoughts were chaotic as she waited. Would Simon see her point of view, or would he, as a doctor, insist on sticking to the rules?

They came back in silence, but as soon as they were seated Simon said abruptly, 'You realise, of course, that I can't sign the death certificate?'

Miss Greenfield did not seem surprised, and it was Wendy who burst out, 'Surely it's obvious that he's dead?'

'Haven't you worked out that there'll have to be a post-mortem?' His tone was impatient, but the look that he gave her was not unsympathetic. 'There may even be an inquest, but I hope, for your sake, it won't be necessary. You'd certainly be required to give evidence.'

Wendy recoiled in alarm. 'I should absolutely hate that!'

'Personally, I don't think it's likely to happen, but it all depends on the post-mortem. The powers that be will want to know what caused him to fall.'

'He'd been strictly forbidden to use the stairs,' Miss Greenfield snapped. 'He may, of course, have slipped, but I think it quite likely he had a heart attack.'

'That would certainly be the best solution from all points of view.' Simon suddenly looked straight at Wendy and this time she couldn't read his expression. 'Whatever the reason for the fall, it's not going to be easy to explain why you didn't immediately send for an ambulance.'

She said bitterly, 'I wish I had!' then went through it laboriously all over again, doing her best to explain that resuscitation had seemed of such terrific importance that she hadn't even thought of anything else.

'It didn't occur to you that an ambulance would have brought specialist equipment and men experienced in handling such cases?'

'I told you—I didn't think about it at all. I—I just got on with the job.' Her chin tilted defiantly, but only her locked hands in her lap prevented her from letting him see she was shaking with nerves inside.

'What you did was perfectly correct—except not getting someone to phone A and E. After all, you had two nurses with you,' he pointed out quietly. 'One could have been spared.'

Wendy had heard it all before from Miss Greenfield, and no repetition could make it sound any better. In the midst of her distress she couldn't help feeling furious with herself for getting into this situation. Nothing she had done, or not done, could have made any difference to poor Mr Mallory—of that she was convinced—but she had been nursing long enough to know how important it was to follow accepted procedure.

What a fool she had been! And how foolish, too, to mind so much because Simon had been involved in her humiliation.

CHAPTER NINE

Simon left Hillside in a very disturbed state of mind. Although he personally was prepared to accept that nothing could have been done to save Mr Mallory's life, he felt far from convinced that the authorities would see the affair in the same light.

So much depended on the result of the post-mortem.

He was not pleased to discover that he had been unwise enough to leave his car under a lime tree, with the result that the bonnet and windscreen were liberally bespotted with greenish-yellow lime flowers and their accompanying stickiness. Muttering a hearty curse, he operated the washers and began a vigorous rubbing with a duster.

Suddenly a young, eager voice spoke from behind. 'Can I help you, Simon?' and he swung round to discover Debra, her bright blue eyes regarding him hopefully.

'Please let me,' she begged.

Simon didn't want any help—he had nearly finished anyway—and he was about to refuse when he remembered that much regretted offer he had made to Wendy. He had promised to have a word with Debra about her relations with Sean, and he couldn't possibly have a better opportunity than the present one.

Yet he was desperate to get back to the hospital, where he had been particularly busy, and the last thing he wanted was a tiresome delay of this sort. Nor was he in any mood to be tactful.

Nevertheless, he found himself handing a spare duster to Debra. For a moment they rubbed in silence, then Simon addressed her abruptly.

'By the way, young Debra, I've been hearing things about you.'

She stopped work and gazed at him, her eyes wide with alarm. 'Like what?'

'Something which could easily get you into serious trouble. It might be a good idea to heed a well meant word of warning.'

For heaven's sake, how ponderous could you get? Disgusted with himself for such a fuddy-duddy approach, Simon laboured on.

'I'm talking about your—er—friendship with Sean Conway. You were seen coming out of his room, after you were supposed to be off duty, in a somewhat over-excited and rumpled state. I'm sure you know that sort of thing just won't do. Miss Greenfield would throw a fit!'

As she listened, Debra's healthy sun-kissed face had turned pale with shock, but now she was suddenly bright red with anger.

'Who saw me?' she demanded.

Not having anticipated the question, Simon had to think rapidly. 'That has nothing whatsoever to do with it,' he said firmly. 'You *were* seen, and that's all you need to know. You're not trying to deny it happened, are you?'

'Of course not!' Debra made a not very successful snatch at her temper. 'I like Sean and he's lonely here, so why shouldn't we get together whenever there's an opportunity? You ought to be glad I was *off* duty instead of using that to make it sound worse. We've had several very interesting conversations during working hours, and that time I stayed late it was for a special reason.'

'Indeed! Am I permitted to know what it was?'

'We were reading a play—Sean's mad about the theatre——'

'What play?' Simon interrupted suspiciously.

'It was Shakespeare, actually. He's a lot more fun than you realise when you have to study him at school. It was something from *The Merchant of Venice.*' For the first time her voice faltered. 'A love scene, as a matter of fact, but—but that doesn't mean we were doing anything we shouldn't.'

Simon looked at her frank, open face and knew he had no option but to believe her, yet he felt impelled to fight a rearguard action.

'And was it the beauty of Shakespeare's words which excited you to such an extent that you emerged looking flushed and doing up the buttons of your dress?'

Debra shrugged and said carelessly, 'I probably was looking flushed. It's a very moving scene, and I felt quite exalted. In fact, I think I might go on the stage instead of being a nurse, but I'm not sure yet.'

'The buttons?' Simon prodded.

'Those stupid button-through dresses we have to wear are always coming undone because the buttonholes are all too big.' Childishly, she added, 'So there!'

'OK, you win.' Simon held out his hand for the duster and put it away with his own. It had been one of the most embarrassing conversations he had ever embarked on, and he was heartily sick of it. It didn't help that he had only himself to blame for getting involved.

He was groping for his seatbelt when Debra hurled herself at the open window.

'Simon! I've just remembered I met Jane when I was coming out of Sean's room and she was ever so cross because I'd kept her waiting. It was *she* who told you, wasn't it?'

'No, it wasn't!' roared Simon. 'I've hardly ever spoken to Jane—and I don't want to hear another word on the subject from you or anybody else. Goodbye!'

His car raced away down the drive, but Debra stood still looking after it with a very thoughtful expression on her face.

Wendy spent the rest of the day in the depths of depression. With uncomfortable vividness she recalled her first interview with Miss Greenfield, when the sister-in-charge had made it plain she was dubious about the applicant's suitability for the post of sister. And now she had been proved right. The fact that Anna had said, 'I'd probably have done the same,' was of little comfort since Wendy was sure it was only a kind heart which had prompted it.

It didn't help her state of mind that she happened to be the one who answered the phone when Simon rang up to say he had arranged for Mr Mallory's body to be removed while the patients were at supper.

'When is the PM?' Wendy asked anxiously.

'Probably tomorrow morning. I'll phone through the result as soon as I know what it is.' He hesitated and his tone changed. 'Keep your chin up, Wendy, love. It was all very unfortunate, but with any luck you'll come out of it all right.'

Her heart had leapt at the casual endearment, but nothing of that showed in her voice as she answered gloomily, 'I probably won't get any luck.'

'Well, of course, if you're determined to look on the black side——'

'You've *made* me look on it—you and Miss Greenfield. You both seemed to think my behaviour had bordered on the criminal when I was only trying to save a man's life.'

'Rubbish!' Simon snapped. 'In my own case I simply had to take the official line, but don't imagine I wasn't sympathetic underneath.'

'Well, all I can say is you hid it extremely well,' Wendy flung back at him wildly.

She had held herself in so tightly all day that her control was beginning to slip. The unexpected softening of Simon's attitude had acted as a catalyst and she was suddenly on the verge of tears. If only she had been at the cottage, she could have given way, but she was still on duty, still Sister McBride no matter how unsuitable she had proved to be.

'I don't think,' Simon was saying calmly, 'that you're in any mood for a rational conversation just now. I only called to tell you about the ambulance.' On the verge of ringing off, he added suddenly, 'Hang on a minute—one more item of information. I had a word with Debra as promised, and the whole affair seems to have been entirely innocent. I'm sure she was telling the truth, so that's one thing less for you to worry about.'

'Oh—er—thank you,' Wendy said faintly. 'I'm very relieved to hear it.'

Jane must have exaggerated the incident, and she had believed her. At that moment it seemed just another example of her inability to choose the right course of action. She should have tackled Debra at once instead of telling Simon about it and then weakly accepting his impulsive offer of help.

Perhaps she was destined to be a fool about everything? She had imagined she wanted to marry Vernon, and it had turned out all wrong. And now she had allowed herself—she might as well admit it—to fall in love with Simon, and this time a deeply rooted instinct assured her it was for real.

Whereas Simon, though obviously attracted to her, merely regarded her as a substitute for Helen, his girlfriend-in-chief.

If only she had never come to Hillside. . . And yet she couldn't possibly be sorry she had met Simon—even if it was bringing her such pain as she had never known before.

Besides, her ankle had been completely cured by the osteopathic treatment, and she owed this to Simon, as well as many small kindnesses such as doing the shopping for Bramble. He must like her quite a bit, she concluded without any satisfaction whatsoever, but she was quite sure he didn't love her.

It would take an emotion much deeper than casual affection to erase the memory of the wife who had been killed so tragically.

Emerging from the office, Wendy looked left and right and then dived into the staff cloakroom. Examining her face in the mirror, she discerned traces of tears, but only because she was looking for them. She didn't think anyone else would notice. Steeling herself to continue with this dreadful day, she went upstairs to begin the early evening drug round.

This always took much longer than the morning round because the patients were scattered all over the house. After locating the last two in the bil-

liard-room, Wendy slipped out to the yard for a
reviving breath of fresh air. Unfortunately this
proved to be a mistake because it landed her with
an embarrassing episode which, on any other day,
she could have taken in her stride.

Debra was there, pumping up the back tyre of
her bicycle preparatory to departing. On seeing
Wendy, the teenager immediately straightened up
and hailed her.

'Sister! Can I speak to you, please?'

'Of course you can.' Smiling, Wendy
approached. 'What's the trouble?'

Debra took a deep breath and went straight to
the point. 'Why did you tell Simon about Jane
seeing me come out of Sean's room? I soon
guessed she was the one who'd been spying, and
I got it out of her that she'd told you. I wouldn't
have minded so much if *you'd* ticked me off, but
I've never been so humiliated in my whole life as I
was when Simon started complaining about my
morals. I do think it was mean of you!' She broke
off and swallowed. 'I'm sorry—I know I shouldn't
speak to a sister like this, but I can't help how I
feel.'

Wendy gazed at her blankly, completely taken
aback at the sudden attack. Why had she told
Simon? As far as she could remember, it had been
a sudden impulse.

'Never mind about my being a sister. I think,
just for the moment, we'd better pretend I'm not.'
She moved nearer and lowered her voice. 'I'm

sorry you were upset about it, but I'm afraid you'll have to accept that it just happened in the course of conversation. I didn't ask him to speak to you, but we both thought you might prefer it to come from him——'

'I can't think why,' Debra interrupted.

'Neither can I now, but I assure you that we did. Perhaps it was something to do with Simon being quite a lot older than you.'

'You're quite old too.'

'Yes, I know.' Wendy repressed a wry smile. 'Anyway, it's all over now, and the sooner it's forgotten, the better. I'm sorry you found it embarrassing, but our intentions were good. If what Jane imagined had been true, you would probably have had to leave Hillside.'

'Really?' Debra seemed genuinely surprised.

'Yes, really. And please don't get yourself into that sort of situation again—in other words, keep out of Sean's room.'

'OK. He'll be going soon anyway.' Debra turned her back and continued her vigorous pumping.

Returning to the house, Wendy reviewed the conversation and knew she ought to be feeling glad that the matter was now cleared up. But somehow gladness was beyond her, and she could only rather drearily add Debra's name to the list of people whose disapproval she had earned today.

It was a relief when her spell of duty ended and she could return to the peace of her little flat, and a welcome from Bramble. After feeding the animal she eventually settled down before the television with it on her lap, and in her mind the firm intention of putting the events of the day on one side so that she could relax before going to bed.

It proved impossible, of course, and she was already tired of her own company when a tap came on the door. Thinking it was Anna, whom she had just heard returning from one of her frequent visits to her family, Wendy jumped up with alacrity.

But it was Simon.

'Oh!' She stared at him, her heart pounding. 'I didn't know it was you.'

'Or you wouldn't have opened the door?'

'Don't be silly!' Her colour deepened. 'I didn't think you would have any reason to call.'

'A very good reason, I assure you. May I come in?'

'Yes, of course.' She held the door wider. 'Coffee?'

'No thanks. This is a professional call. In other words, I've come to check up on last night's surgery.' Simon crossed the room to where the cat sat watching him with wide green eyes.

'Was it really only last night? It seems ages ago.' Wendy closed the door and came to join him. 'Bramble seems to have kept the bandage on very well, but of course, she hasn't been outside yet.'

'She?'

'I've made up my mind she's female. For one thing, she's small-made and I think she has an air of femininity, so that's what she's going to be until I'm proved wrong—which I hope won't happen.'

'I'm a great believer in feminine intuition,' Simon said solemnly, his eyes on the bandaged paw.

'I think it works sometimes,' Wendy agreed. 'But certainly not always.'

It hadn't worked for her when she had been attracted to Vernon, nor when she had applied for the job at Hillside. No premonition had warned her what getting to know Simon would do to her heart.

He was making sure with gentle fingers that the makeshift splint was still in position. Looking at his downbent head, Wendy noticed that the thick reddish-brown hair needed cutting. The ends curled behind his ears and along the edge of his collar, and she had trouble in resisting the temptation to touch.

'I know I'm overdue at the barber's,' Simon said unexpectedly.

She flushed and withdrew slightly, almost as though she had been caught in the act of feeling the crisp, bright hair. 'I don't expect you get much time for that sort of thing,' she remarked hastily.

'Time enough if I organised myself better, but I'd always rather play squash, or do something energetic out of doors.' He changed the subject abruptly. 'Are you feeling better now you've had a bit of peace and quiet?'

'Talk about intuition!' Wendy tried to laugh.

'That is a superb example of the masculine variety. How did you know I was in need of peace?'

'You've had a hellish day, and I know you've been feeling unhappy because of the way you talked on the phone. If you really want to know, it was as much to check up on you as on the cat that I came to call.'

Wendy could think of nothing to say and, quite without warning, she felt tears welling up in her eyes. At the convalescent home she had managed to control them, but here there wasn't the same necessity. Helplessly, she allowed them to fall.

'Oh, my dear——' Simon put his arms round her and cradled her head against his chest.

She felt him rest his chin gently on the top of her head and the thudding of his heart was loud in her ears. It was utter bliss—in spite of her tears—to feel herself wrapped round with sympathy and—what? Certainly not love, but something she could momentarily pretend resembled the warm, deep emotion she craved. The fact that she dwelt in a fool's paradise—and knew it—was something that she could, for a few minutes, forget.

Her tears were drying fast, but she still kept her face hidden against the shirt she had soaked, prolonging briefly the erotic pleasure of feeling his arms holding her tight.

'Poor Wendy,' Simon said softly. 'I think things have rather caught up with you, haven't they?'

'Things?' She raised her head and peered at him through sodden lashes.

'You came here so soon after the accident, and with your injured ankle a constant reminder. You were shattered by your fiancé's death and in no state to begin an entirely new job. I hoped you were gradually growing less vulnerable, but today has shown you're still far too sensitive for coping with disasters.'

Wendy jerked herself free as indignation dried her eyes. How dared he talk to her as though she were an invalid! She couldn't possibly tell him the true cause of her distress, but at least she could snatch at this opportunity of putting him right about Vernon.

'Listen a minute.' She stood holding on to the back of a chair, as though it could give her moral as well as physical support. 'It's true I was shattered when I came here, but it wasn't because my heart was broken. Before the accident happened, Vernon and I had admitted that the engagement had been a dreadful mistake. We were naturally disappointed but not emotionally upset—in fact, what we both felt was relief. Then he was killed. I felt awful, of course, but not in the way everybody imagined, and it made it worse having to pretend to family and friends that I'd suffered a tragic bereavement.'

Simon was looking puzzled. 'Surely you could have told the people who were closest to you?'

But Wendy shook her head. 'When somebody

you're supposed to love very much dies unexpectedly, you simply can't go around saying it was all a mistake and you didn't love him at all. It's just not possible. In the circumstances, I thought it best and safest not to tell *anybody*.'

He stood staring at her blankly, and the sudden silence was broken only by the purring of the cat and the twittering of sleepy birds beyond the open window.

'So why are you telling *me*?' he asked.

'Because I was getting sympathy under false pretences.' She hesitated, then continued, 'It's not the first time I've felt that with you. That evening soon after I came to Hillside, when you told me about losing your wife, you assumed I'd suffered similarly, and I felt a terrible hypocrite because I hadn't. But you didn't give me a chance to explain.'

Looking at him intently, Wendy saw the birth of a smile in the tawny depths of his eyes.

'I remember that evening. I made rather a fool of myself, and you were very sweet.'

'You'd had a little too much whisky on top of being absolutely worn out,' she said gently.

'It's kind of you to say so.'

She made a small gesture of dismissal and they were silent for a moment.

Then Simon said slowly, 'Now that you've told me all this, I can't quite understand why you were knocked for six by the aftermath of Mallory's death. It was distressing for you to feel yourself criticised, I agree, but it seemed to me you were exaggerating the whole thing. I admit we don't yet know the result of the PM——'

'No, we don't!' Biting her lip, Wendy struggled for control. 'Sometimes things do affect you more than others,' she went on more calmly, 'and perhaps I was extra tired. Whatever the reason, I really was feeling terribly depressed when you came, and I'm grateful to you for putting up with me—even if you did talk to me like a Dutch uncle!' Somehow she managed a smile.

'It was a pleasure,' Simon said politely. 'Any time you want a shoulder to cry on, mine is available—provided I'm here, of course.'

They both laughed, though there was not much mirth in it. At the door, he paused with his hand on the knob.

'Don't forget there's a fête committee on Friday evening. They'll be finalising the arrangements, so I suppose we'd better both turn up if we can.'

Wendy had forgotten the existence of the fête committee. Immediately there flashed into her mind a vivid memory of what had happened after a previous one. She and Simon had wandered by the lake and had that ridiculous conversation about moorhens and coots. Other things had happened too, but she preferred not to think about that. They mustn't happen again.

'It's my free weekend,' she told him, and added on an impulse, 'I thought of going home.'

'On Friday night?'

'Why not? There's a train about nine o'clock. If I catch that I could have forty-eight hours instead of only a day and a half——'

'So you could,' he agreed. 'Are you taking the cat with you?'

'Oh!' Wendy looked conscience-stricken. 'I'd forgotten all about Bramble. How awful of me!'

'Not awful at all. That sort of thing is likely to happen when people make snap decisions.'

She would have liked to hit him, but she restrained herself. 'My mother's always urging me to visit them, so it wasn't really a snap decision. Anyway, I don't see how you could tell.'

'My dear, it was perfectly obvious you only thought of it as an excuse for dodging the committee. However, as you won't be able to leave Bramble until she's settled in, it looks as though you'll have to do without your trip home.'

He left with no more than a casual goodnight. Leaning back against the closed door, Wendy allowed a long, quivering sigh to escape her. It had seemed so sensible to put as much distance as possible between herself and Simon during her off-duty time, and now her plan had been thwarted by one small cat with a bandaged paw.

Picking the little animal up, she buried her face in the soft fur. She would have to think of some other way, that was all.

Unfortunately, as she knew perfectly well in her secret heart, it was already much too late.

* * *

The atmosphere at Hillside the following morning was tense, though the patients were unaware of it. Several of them referred to Mr Mallory's death, heaping praise on Sister McBride and Nurse Johnson for their efforts at resuscitation. Wendy found this uncomfortable and, as a result, earned further good marks for modesty.

Although she knew they were unlikely to get the result of the post-mortem before mid-morning at the earliest, every time she happened to be near enough to the office to hear the phone ring she had to battle with the temptation to eavesdrop. It would have been easier if it had been her turn to take surgery. That, at least, would have occupied her thoughts to the exclusion of everything else.

At coffee time Miss Greenfield avoided the subject, and the conversation dwelt mostly on the coming fête.

'It's something I dread each year,' the sister-in-charge confessed. 'I know the friends work very hard and deserve our wholehearted support, but most of the money raised goes to the City Hospital and not Hillside.' She addressed Wendy. 'You can't conceive of the mess and muddle we have to contend with on fête day! One year it rained and we had to have all the stalls indoors, with most of the outside entertainments cancelled. The whole house was turned into absolute bedlam.'

'We all survived,' Anna pointed out cheerfully.

'True—but only just! I don't think I shall ever forget that year.'

They went on talking, and Wendy continued to make suitable replies, but the telephone was silent all through the coffee break, and she had to return to work with tension unrelieved.

It was nearly lunchtime when Simon rang up.

CHAPTER TEN

WENDY was in the office alone when the phone rang. She had just unlocked the drugs cupboard to get some paracetamol for a patient who had complained of a headache. The bottle, she remembered, was on the bottom shelf and she located it without difficulty, but the sound of the telephone froze her into immobility.

She had no reason to guess that this time it just had to be Simon, but somehow she felt sure it was, and she actually wished that Miss Greenfield had been there so that she wouldn't have to do anything.

This was ridiculous. Wendy put the bottle down on the desk and reached across to pick up the handset.

'Hillside.'

Her voice had come out in such a strange croak that Simon didn't recognise it. He said briskly, 'Dr Meadows here. Can I speak to Miss Greenfield or one of the sisters, please?'

'It's Wendy. Have—have you——'

'Yes, I have, if you're referring to the PM report.'

What else could she possibly be talking about? Controlling her impatience with difficulty, Wendy confirmed it, but she couldn't help adding,

'Don't mess about, Simon, *please*! Give it to me straight.'

'OK.' His voice sounded as though he were smiling. 'Well, you've got nothing to worry about, love. Mallory died of cardiac arrest——'

'We knew that.'

'Yes, but it was a massive heart attack which caused him to fall. Theoretically, you were at fault in not sending for an ambulance at once, but nobody has suggested you should be disciplined for it, so there's really no need for you to give it another thought.' He paused, then added, as Wendy was speechless, 'Does that make you feel better?'

'Oh, *yes*!' Her voice had come back to her filled with bubbling excitement. 'And Miss Greenfield will be pleased too. She's been very worried in case Hillside was criticised. Do you want to speak to her?'

'There's no need. You can have the pleasure of telling her the good news. Be seeing you.'

Returning the handset to its rest, Wendy was about to make a dash for the door when she remembered her reason for being in the office at that particular moment. Snatching up the bottle of paracetamol, she tipped two capsules into a tiny saucer and locked the remainder in the drugs cupboard. After dosing her patient she went in search of the sister-in-charge.

Miss Greenfield received the news with outward

calm, but she could not conceal a heartfelt sigh of relief.

'I must admit I'm thankful to have this unfortunate incident cleared up so satisfactorily. Hillside has never had anything of the kind happen before—not in my time, anyway—and the good reputation of the home is very close to my heart. I expect you were worried too.'

'Yes, I was,' Wendy admitted. 'In fact, I was scared stiff.'

'Then let this be a warning to you. Always handle a situation correctly in accordance with medical custom and no one can criticise you.' Miss Greenfield paused, evidently debating something in her mind, then continued, 'I was particularly sorry you were involved, because I've been extremely pleased with the way you've settled down at Hillside. You may remember I thought you a little young for the post, but you've tackled it remarkably well, and I'm sure the patients have every confidence in you.

Wendy flushed with pleasure. 'Thank you, Miss Greenfield. I've been very happy here.'

It was true—up to a point. But the discovery of what Simon had done to her heart had altered the whole situation.

That evening, as she walked slowly down the drive, she tried to face up to what the future held for her. Was she to continue her planned avoidance of Simon in spite of the difficulties caused by living in the same house? He would be sure to notice it sooner or later. After all, she hadn't exactly discouraged his attentions in the past!

So what was the alternative?

The only one she could think of was to leave Hillside, and that wouldn't be easy after the praise she had just received. Besides, she didn't want to go away. She liked the convalescent home itself and the beauty of its surroundings, and she loved her attractive flatlet.

Oblivious of the lovely summer evening, Wendy frowned as she piled all these attractions on to one side of her mental scales, and on the other she put just one thing—the misery of loving a man who looked on her as a casual girlfriend. There was absolutely no doubt about the result. The scales went down with a bang on the wrong side.

Unless she was a glutton for punishment, she would have to get away, but she needn't face up to it quite yet. Not until after the the fête.

There was a committee meeting on Friday, she remembered, and since her visit home had been proved impracticable she would have no excuse for not attending.

When Friday came, she took her place round the table with the others, and was relieved to hear Simon's apologies being read out. He had been unavoidably detained at the hospital, so now she could relax and give her mind to the business in hand.

She learnt more about her own role. Although her base would be the table where the raffle prizes were displayed, she would also be expected to make sorties among the crowd, ensuring that everyone bought a ticket, or preferably a whole strip of tickets. She hoped she wouldn't make a fool of herself by asking the same people twice.

'All we need now is a fine day,' the chairman said at the end of the meeting. 'We're usually lucky, so you must all keep your fingers crossed.'

The day before the fête it rained, and the patients told each other that it would be all the more likely to be fine next day, and the rain would 'freshen up the flowerbeds wonderfully'. Friends of the hospital making preliminary arrangements for the side-shows and stalls cursed the weather, the soaking wet grass, and the impossibility of leaving any thing which would spoil out overnight.

Fortunately the patients were proved right. The night nurse, who cared nothing for fêtes and would be going home to her bed as usual, saw the sun rise quietly behind a delicate veil of mist. Soon its rays were making the raindrops sparkle and then vanish on leaves and flowers. Paths and lawns dried rapidly, and by ten o'clock it hardly seemed possible that the downpour had appeared so unrelenting only yesterday.

Cars swept up the drive bringing eager workers, and the grounds near the house became a hive of activity. The ballet mistress arrived in her Metro to inspect the grass and decide if she could allow her pupils to perform. To everyone's relief—for child

dancers were always a great draw—she concluded
it was perfectly feasible.

Simon had suggested the dancers, Wendy
remembered. Would he be there to see them in
action?

She and Anna were—theoretically—both on
duty all day, but this only meant that they were
obliged to wear uniform instead of putting on
pretty summer dresses. They would be busy as
usual in the house all the morning, but in the
afternoon they could perform their allotted tasks
out of doors, provided they were on hand if
needed medically.

As soon as lunch was over, Anna went off to the
bookstall in the yard and Wendy began to sell
raffle tickets to the patients and helpers long before
the fête was officially opened by the Mayoress.
Simon, she knew, had kept himself free from
duties of any kind, but she felt sure he would put
in an appearance if he could. In the midst of
tearing off tickets and counting change, she found
herself watching for his tall, athletic figure thread-
ing its way through the crowds, but there was no
sign of him.

Perhaps he was waiting for Helen to be off duty
and able to accompany him?

The crowded scene was a colourful one, filled
with chatter and laughter, the excited cries of
children and powerful musical items from the
Stourwell Silver Band. Everyone seemed happy,
and Wendy—who had done her utmost to fling

herself into the spirit of the occasion—suddenly felt she could bear it no longer. To get completely out of earshot would be impossible, but she simply *had* to distance herself from it all for a short time— if only to stop that stupid, hopeless search for Simon's copper-brown head.

Yet she hesitated, knowing she was supposed to remain on duty with her raffle tickets, and at that moment the lady in charge came unwittingly to her rescue.

'Sales seem to be slacking off a bit now. Why don't you go and get yourself some tea?'

Wendy thanked her gratefully and slipped away. As she paused, wondering which way to go, the music stopped abruptly and the voice of the chairman came over the Tannoy.

'Has anybody seen a little fair-haired boy named Robin? He's four years old and wearing red shorts and a top to match. He's been missing for nearly ten minutes and his parents are anxious. Anybody finding him please report to me here outside the french windows.'

Wendy remembered seeing the child, but it was some while ago. He had been trying to climb a tree and, as she wondered how best to stop him, his mother came up and soon put an end to it. She had liked the impish, freckled little face and was distressed to hear he was missing.

But no doubt someone would soon find him and return him to his parents.

Why shouldn't that person be herself? She

wasn't so much in need of a cuppa that she was prepared to queue up for it, and a solitary walk in a quieter part of the park still seemed a much more attractive alternative. And so, picking a path at random, she began to stroll casually away from the crowded lawns, scanning her surroundings as she walked for a flash of bright red.

Unfortunately the path was leading her straight towards a clump of trees where a man and a girl had also withdrawn from the crowd. They lay in each other's arms, oblivious of an onlooker, totally absorbed in themselves.

Wendy didn't grudge them their enjoyment of each other. She just didn't want to look at it.

Veering off in a different direction, she suddenly realised her new path was taking her towards the lake. Unconsciously she quickened her steps as it occurred to her that the missing Robin was very likely the kind of little boy to be attracted by that sort of place.

Before long she saw the glint of shimmering water, blue like the sky, and soon she was walking beside it, her eyes darting hither and thither. She passed the seat where she had sat with Simon that magic evening and went on to where the reeds and rushes grew profusely, almost hiding the water. The ducks were making a lot of noise and swimming up and down with no apparent purpose. Maybe they could see something she couldn't?

Wendy slowed down and began to peer among

the greenery, and suddenly she saw the flash of red for which she had been looking. It was the merest glimpse, but a little farther on the rushes were lower, pushed aside by a fallen tree, and here she got a better view.

It was a slender tree, projecting over the water for about ten feet and gradually sloping down until the end was only a few inches above the surface of the lake. About halfway along the spot of red turned into a small boy carefully edging himself forward, his sturdy little body rigid with concentration.

Her hunch had paid off, and she had found the missing Robin.

Keeping out of sight in case she startled the child and caused him to lose his balance, Wendy debated what to do. He was having a wonderful adventure and would certainly be unwilling to relinquish it at the bidding of an unknown female. Besides, if she called out suddenly, it would be even more startling then merely appearing from nowhere.

He had nearly reached the end now and would have to tackle the hazardous return journey. Since it was impossible for her to help him, perhaps she had better keep quiet, holding herself in readiness in case something awful happened.

To her horror Robin had now discovered that bouncing up and down made the trunk behave like a sort of trampoline, and he was enjoying it enormously. Next he pretended it was a horse, shouting encouragement to what was clearly a mettlesome steed.

This was more dangerous than ever and had got to be stopped. Sick with dread, Wendy realised she would have to risk a shout.

But she was too late. The tapering end of the tree, unable to bear even such a small weight any longer, snapped. With a scream of terror the child was catapulted into the water. There was a splash which frightened the ducks, then nothing except a widening circle of ripples.

Wendy opened her mouth and shrieked as loudly as she could, 'Help! Help!' though unless someone happened to be quite near she had no hope of being heard above the noise of the fête. Then she tore off her shoes and—rather absurdly, she thought afterwards—snatched her sister's frilly cap from her head and tossed it into the rushes. It was easy to slide down the low bank, but the moment her feet encountered watery mud and a tangle of roots her difficulties began. Every step was a huge effort as weeds and mud combined to impede her and the rushes barred her path, giving her only glimpses of what was happening ahead.

She saw the little fair head reappear and then go down again, arms flailing wildly. Desperately she struggled on, and at last the water grew deeper and she was able to start swimming.

Impeded by a sodden skirt, she made slow progress, unhappily aware that she wasn't clear of the weeds. They wound themselves round her legs, as slimy and sinuous as snakes, and did their utmost to drag her down to the murky depths below the surface.

Robin's struggles had taken him farther away, but he was tiring now and almost within reach. Making a supreme effort, Wendy stretched out and seized him by the back of his T-shirt. There was a dreadful moment of panic as she fought to avoid his clutching hands and turn him into the correct position for rescue.

Quite suddenly the little body went limp and she knew, with a cold, sick feeling of horror, that she must make that nightmare return journey as fast as she possibly could.

Afterwards she thought it might have been better to make for a different spot, where the lake was free of rushes, even though it would have meant a longer swim, but she automatically turned to go back the way she had come. It was incredible how heavy a four-year-old could seem, but it wasn't so bad while she could still swim. When she was obliged to struggle to her feet, with the child in her arms, the battle with mud and weeds was almost beyond her. Gasping for breath, her face mud-streaked and her body dripping with green slime, she plodded on.

She was so absorbed in her efforts that she didn't notice there were people running along the lakeside path. All she knew was that, quite unexpectedly, help came.

A man had plunged into the filthy mixture of water and mud, regardless of his cream-coloured summer trousers and silk shirt, and was wading towards her at a much greater speed than Wendy could have achieved even unimpeded.

Bewildered, incredulous, she recognised Simon.

He took Robin from her, cradled him in one arm and held out the other hand to assist her. 'Come on, love,' he encouraged her. 'You've almost made it.'

She could have climbed Everest if he was holding her hand. Or so she felt at that moment.

The mud made one last effort to retain its grip on her feet, but Wendy was unbeatable now. In a moment she had scrambled up the bank and was joining Simon on her knees beside the child who, covered with mud, lay dreadfully still and quiet between them.

People were crowding round, among them Robin's frantic parents, but Simon ordered them to stand back and, recognising the voice of authority, they obeyed. He put the little boy in the recovery position and began the battle for his life. The small group of onlookers fell silent and even the ducks were quiet. At a distance the noise of the fête continued unabated, and it seemed to Wendy they were all isolated in a tiny world of their own where they had nothing to do but wait.

For what seemed an eternity—though it was probably less that a minute—Simon appeared to be achieving nothing at all. Then there was a sudden convulsive movement of the small chest and Robin coughed. A stream of muddy water poured from his mouth and safely away into the grass. His eyes half opened and he gave a strangled cry.

'Mummy! I want my mummy!'

'Here I am, darling!' A dark girl burst out of the crowd and flung herself on her knees beside him, tears streaming down her face. She would have gathered her child up into her arms had Simon not stopped her.

'Just a moment.' He put his fingers on the little boy's wrist, waited briefly, then nodded. 'OK, he's all yours. Have you got something to wrap him in? It's important he should be warmed up as soon as possible, provided it's done with care.'

'There's a rug in the car.' Her husband leaned over her, and Wendy could see he was near to tears himself.

He took off his lightweight jacket and put it round his little son as he snuggled into his mother's arms, ruining her white dress. 'I wonder if we can get back to the car park a different way,' he went on. 'We don't want to walk through all the crowds looking like this and everbody staring and wondering what's happened.'

'It's quite easy.' Simon gave them swift directions.

They thanked him profusely, adding more fervent thanks as they suddenly remembered he had just brought their child back to life.

'I merely finished the job off,' he reminded them, indicating Wendy, who was sitting on the ground feeling more cold and tired than she had ever done before. 'She's the one who really deserves your gratitude.'

They were only too willing to say thank you all over again, but she was so weary she scarcely seemed to have the strength to make a suitable reply. All that really mattered, it appeared to her, was that a terrible tragedy had been averted. Her only requirement now was a long, long soak in a hot bath, but further effort had to be made before she could achieve that. Making a supreme effort, she hauled herself to her feet, clinging to a branch of the fallen tree.

It was very strange. Although her limbs seemed to be weighted down with lead, her head felt extraordinarily light. A well known face swam in front of her, though most of the spectators had left, and with an effort she recognised it as Debra's. She was saying something, but Wendy didn't seem to be able to hear what it was.

Then, over the teenager's shoulder, she glimpsed another familiar face among the very few people who still lingered. This one was quite different—beautiful rather than merely attractive, with regular features, deep blue eyes and a lot of blonde hair. With no trouble at all, Wendy gave a name to it. Helen Barber.

The cream, pink and gold vision blurred before her eyes. She swayed and nearly fell back into the rushes. As Simon put out his hand to steady her, her legs gave way completely and she collapsed into a heap on the bank.

For the first time in her life she had fainted.

When Wendy returned to consciousness, she couldn't at first make out what was happening. She was staring down at grass, but she certainly wasn't walking over it in spite of being bumped along at a good speed. She tried to move her legs, but something was preventing them from responding, and her slight effort caused the grip to tighten.

'Sorry about this,' came Simon's voice. 'It's not very elegant, I know, but it's much the easiest way to transport an inert body.'

Not much caring for the description of herself, Wendy forced her bewildered mind to start functioning again. She was being carried over Simon's shoulder like a sack of garden rubbish, and it was most uncomfortable as well as being extremely undignified.

'Put me down!' She hammered on his back with her fists. 'Put me down *at once!*'

'I shall have to if you're going to carry on like that.' He stopped and allowed her to slip to the ground. 'Sure you feel up to walking? It's not far now, but——'

'Not far to where?' she asked stupidly.

'The cottage, of course.'

She halted and looked around, trying to gauge

where they were. The fête was still going strong,
and not very far away either, but the spot they
had reached was deserted and quiet. Just behind
those trees, she calculated, they would come to
the drive and then the cottage.

Simon took her arm and hurried her along.
Wishing her legs didn't feel so much like bundles
of limp rag, she was glad of his help.

'I fainted, didn't I?' she said. 'Why didn't you
just leave me lying there? I'd have come round in
due course.'

'I was afraid you'd get a severe chill in those
soaking wet clothes, and with your bodily
defences at a low ebb. The sooner you're warm
and dry the better.'

A loud voice came over the Tannoy, telling
people it was their last chance to buy raffle tickets,
and Wendy was suddenly conscience-stricken.

'I must get bathed and into fresh clothes as
quickly as I can. At least I shall be able to help
with the clearing up.'

'You'll do no such thing!' Simon was at his most
dogmatic. 'You've had an appalling experience
and need time to recover.' He looked down at her
disgusting state. 'Come to think of it, it'll take you
some time to get respectable again. I reckon the
fête will be over and done with by the time you're
fit to reappear.'

They had reached the cottage, and Wendy had
never been so glad to see her home. She was
shivering now, with reaction as well as cold, and

it was as much as she could do to haul herself up the stairs.

Simon had disappeared into his own flat, but he appeared again as she was fumbling with her key, a glass containing a small quantity of whisky in his hand. He took the key from her, unlocked the door and presented her with the glass.

'Doctor's orders.'

Wendy took it unwillingly, then, meeting his uncompromising stare, took a few small sips. The fiery liquid slid down her throat and seemed to spread a glow all over her cold body.

'I've just remembered something,' she said suddenly. 'The people at the raffle table will wonder what's happened to me. When you go back, could you explain to them, please? You'd better tell Anna too, if you come across her.'

'Will do.' He stood in the doorway, studying her intently. 'Is there anything else I can do for you? If you don't feel up to undressing, I'll gladly help——'

'I'll manage.' A thought which had been hovering at the back of her mind suddenly burst through to the front. 'By the way, how did you happen to turn up just in time to take Robin from me?'

'I heard your cry for help, though I didn't know it was your voice, of course. I was standing on the edge of the crowd, talking to his parents, as a matter of fact, along with a few other people. We all heard it, but nobody was sure of the direction because the sound was so faint. We inevitably wasted a bit of time arguing about it. Then I thought of the lake, and it seemed the best place to start.'

No doubt Helen had been one of the 'other people', and she would be waiting for him now, wondering what on earth was keeping him.

Thank you.' Quite suddenly Wendy was at the end of her tether. 'And now, Simon, will you please *go*?'

He gave her a startled look and backed out into the corridor. She thought she heard him say, 'I'll be back later,' then decided she had been mistaken.

He would be spending the rest of the evening with Helen. Of course he would.

CHAPTER ELEVEN

WENDY lay back in the steaming, scented water and half closed her eyes. She had been generous with the bath oil and its perfume had overcome the odour of lake mud emanating from the pile of filthy clothes on the floor. She was no longer shaking, no longer cold—physically she felt great.

Mentally she was utterly miserable.

Hadn't she made some sort of promise to herself that she would tackle the problem of her future when the fête was over? Well, it was over now, or as good as. No doubt Simon, after showering and changing his clothes, had resumed his interrupted tour of the attractions with Helen and they were now doing—what?

Lying together in the park like that couple Wendy had seen? Or perhaps off somewhere to a candlelit dinner tête-à-tête?

She sighed and sat up reluctantly. She had been in the bath for nearly an hour, occasionally replenishing the hot water, and she felt so relaxed that every movement was an unwelcome exertion. Her hair dripped in a chilly sort of way over her warm shoulders and she remembered she would now have to shampoo it properly or it would look a mess tomorrow. Making a huge effort, she stood up and reached for the bath towel.

Ten minutes later, clean and dry from top to toe, and with her hair combed into some sort of order, she was searching in her tiny airing cupboard for fresh clothing. Just a bra and pants would do, she decided, and over them she would wear her blue velour caftan. No point in getting dressed properly.

She had just finished her toilet by spraying herself liberally with scent and was sitting by the window with Bramble on her lap when there was a knock on the door. For a moment she couldn't move; then somehow she managed to rise and cross the room to open it.

Anna stood outside.

'Just thought I really must come and see if the Hillside heroine was all right after her experience.' She smiled, scanning Wendy's blue-clad figure. 'I must say you look squeaky clean—quite blooming, in fact!'

'I'm OK. But how on earth did you hear about it?'

'My dear, the whole fête knew! Everybody heard the announcement about the boy being missing, and afterwards the chairman told us over the Tannoy about the rescue. He said one of the sisters had found him and saved his life, and I knew it wasn't me.'

'Gosh!' Wendy exclaimed. 'I'm glad I escaped all the fuss.'

'Lavinia knows it was you, and she asked me to congratulate you on your swimming ability and courage.'

It was impossible not to be pleased about that. Perhaps it would help to make up for her incorrect behaviour when Mr Mallory fell downstairs.

Anna was a comforting visitor to have just now, and Wendy asked her to come in and have some coffee. 'Or supper,' she added, 'if you haven't eaten yet.'

'No, thanks. I had a snack when I came in and now I'm going straight to bed. I'm dead on my feet. Helping with a fête's a lot more tiring than nursing!' She laughed, waved her hand in farewell and disappeared into her own flat.

Disconsolate, Wendy wandered back to the window, uncertain whether to bother about a little supper, or copy Anna's example and go to bed. Not caring very much one way or the other made a decision difficult. She was still debating it when there was another knock on her door.

If it wasn't Anna again—and that seemed most unlikely—there was only one other person it could be. Simon.

She was such a long time gathering her courage to open the door that the knock came again, and this time she rose hastily. Simon wasn't easily thwarted, as she had learnt from experience, and it was better to get it over and find out what he wanted. After all, she didn't have to invite him in.

Simon didn't wait to be asked. He came in.

For a moment his eyes raked the curves of her body outlined by the soft caftan. 'You look very fetching, I must say. A great deal more attractive than when I saw you last.' He wrinkled his nose. 'You smell nicer too.'

'I felt I needed something to get rid of the horrible smell of mud. Did you come here just to make comments on my appearance?' she added.

'I told you I'd be coming back.'

'I wasn't sure I'd heard you correctly, and I still don't understand why you've come.'

There was a brief silence, then Simon said quietly, 'Partly to make sure you were all right.'

'Of course I am.' Partly? What did he mean? 'It was stupid of me to faint, but I suppose I was terribly exhausted and—and overwrought. Anyway, I soon got over it, and a hot bath restored me completely.'

'Good.' He stood in the middle of the room, dominating it utterly. 'Aren't you going to ask me to sit down?'

'You don't usually need to be asked.'

'Perhaps I'm on my best behaviour,' he suggested lightly, but, looking at him, Wendy was surprised to see his eyes were very serious indeed.

When she had offered him one of the armchairs, she perched on the arm of another, hoping it would convey the impression that she wasn't expecting a long visit. For a few minutes they chatted idly, mostly about the fête, but their sentences were awkward, lurching from one to another without any of their usual fluency.

Simon told her about the rescue being broadcast over the Tannoy and she interrupted impatiently.

'I know all about that—Anna told me. She called briefly a little while ago, but she didn't come in.'

'I rather get the impression,' Simon said slowly, 'that you would rather I hadn't. Am I right?'

'I—I wasn't expecting it.' Wendy hesitated, but a strange recklessness seemed to have come over her. 'I thought you'd be anxious to get back to Helen.'

His eyebrows shot up. 'Helen?'

'Isn't she your Number One girlfriend?'

For a moment Simon seemed too thunderstruck for speech. Then he leapt to his feet and burst out furiously, 'No, she's bloody well not! What the hell gave you that idea?'

Wendy stared up into his angry face. 'Ever since I came here people have been telling me about Helen, and I haven't heard that she's been demoted and—er—replaced by someone else.'

'For God's sake—you surely didn't need to be told! I thought I'd made it obvious.'

Her heart was thudding, but somehow she managed to preserve an appearance of calm. 'Are you by any chance saying that I'm supposed to be the current holder of the title?'

'Yes, of course—I mean, no!' He ran his fingers through his hair, making it stand on end. With an immense effort he recovered his self-control.

'I don't want you for a girlfriend, Wendy. You're much, much more important to me that that.' His voice dropped to a low note of great tenderness. 'I love you, and I've been wanting to tell you for quite a while, but you never gave me a chance. I came here tonight absolutely determined to say it, no matter what sort of reception I got. And I must say,' he added bitterly, 'it seems I could hardly have chosen a worse time.'

Wendy had heard only three words—'I love you.' But somehow she couldn't—or daren't—believe she had heard aright. Simon was still in love with his wife, wasn't he? He had made that plain soon after she arrived at Hillside. She had understood about his need to have a girlfriend, and might even have been willing to play the role—in a mild sort of way—had she not been so crazy as to let herself fall in love with him.

And now he was telling her she hadn't been crazy at all.

'I don't understand,' she said faintly. 'I thought——'

'You thought I'd go on forever cherishing my broken heart?'

'Not exactly, but you loved Susie so much, and ——' Her voice died away.

'And now I'm saying I love *you*?' His tone deepened with feeling. 'It's true, my darling, and you're the one who's worked the miracle. I shall always think of Susie in a special sort of way, but I'm ready to go forward now and put the past behind me. I can truthfully say the wound is healed.'

He put his hands on her shoulders and let them slide down her back, drawing her closer. Beneath the silky softness of the caftan, her bare flesh thrilled to the pressure of his fingers.

Now, at last, she understood and believed.

After a while she remembered something. 'I saw Helen just before I fainted. I thought she was with you.'

'Far from it. She was with a new boyfriend and they happened to be in the little group who heard your cry for help. That's how she came to be a spectator.' Simon's arms tightened. 'Don't let's talk about her.'

Wendy was only too glad to acquiesce. 'I can think of lots more interesting subjects.'

'And one in particular. You.'

'Me?'

'I still don't know about *your* feelings,' he pointed out gently. 'And I've been very disturbed lately because I sensed you were trying to withdraw from what I'd believed to be a developing relationship. I was terribly afraid you didn't want us to get serious.'

Wendy drew a deep breath. This must be the moment of truth.

'You were quite right about my withdrawing, and utterly wrong about the reason.' She tilted her head back and looked fearlessly into his eyes. 'As soon as I realised I was falling in love with you, I got scared because I didn't want to get hurt. It never occurred to me *you* might be serious too.' On tiptoe she flung her arms round his neck and drew his face down to hers. 'Oh, Simon darling, I've been so dreadfully unhappy! I was even considering leaving Hillside——'

'My poor Wendy.' He kissed her passionately. 'The last thing.I'd ever have wanted was to make you unhappy.'

Their lips clung again, tasting the sweetness of declared love, then Simon broke free for a moment.

'There's just one thing, my dearest love. You will marry me, won't you? If you'd rather we lived together for a little while, I'd go along with that for your sake, but it's not what I really want.'

'It's not what I want either,' Wendy told him fondly. 'Of course I'll marry you. I can't think of anything I'd rather do.'

They both burst out.laughing, delirious with happiness, then passion swept over them. Discovering the zip of her caftan, Simon pulled it down, gazing with delight at the scraps of clothing she wore beneath. His exploring hands slid inside, gently and sensuously caressing her bare skin and sending tingles of ecstasy all over her.

She felt her whole body melting towards him and knew a rapture she had never experienced before. The long, awful day was over and so, too, was the wonderful evening which had followed it.

Now the night was theirs, and they had a lot of wasted time to make up for, but it didn't matter, because they had all their lives in which to love each other.

— MEDICAL ❤ ROMANCE —

The books for enjoyment this month are:

BEYOND HEAVEN AND EARTH Sara Burton
SISTER AT HILLSIDE Clare Lavenham
IN SAFE HANDS Margaret O'Neill
STORM IN PARADISE Judith Worthy

❤   ❤   ❤   ❤   ❤

Treats in store!

Watch next month for the following absorbing stories:

PLAYING THE JOKER Caroline Anderson
ROMANCE IN BALI Margaret Barker
SURGEON'S STRATEGY Drusilla Douglas
HEART IN JEOPARDY Patricia Robertson